MATED TO THE BERSERKERS

A MÉNAGE SHIFTER ROMANCE

LEE SAVINO

SIGN UP TO LEE'S NEWSLETTER

FREE BOOK

THE COMPLETE BERSERKER SAGA

For over a hundred years, the Berserker warriors have fought and killed for kings. There is but one enemy we cannot defeat: the beast within.

The Berserker Saga

Sold to the Berserkers
Mated to the Berserkers
Bred by the Berserkers (FREE novella only available at
www.leesavino.com)
Taken by the Berserkers
Given to the Berserkers
Claimed by the Berserkers

MATED TO THE BERSERKERS

A Highlander and Viking claim their woman...
For over a hundred years, the Berserker warriors have fought and
killed for kings. There is but one enemy we cannot defeat: the
beast within.

A witch told us of the one who can save us--a woman marked by
the wolf. We found and claimed her. But will she accept us as
mates? Can she soothe our feral nature before it is too late?

Highland werewolf Daegan never expected to defeat the
curse of his bloodline. But when a prophecy tells of a
woman who might cure his Berserker rage, he and his
Viking warrior brother will stop at nothing to claim her.

They bring her to their mountain home and train her
according to pack rules. She is their captive; they will never
let her go. For only she can save them before the Berserker
curse destroys them all...

*

A dark fantasy romance... Mated to the Berserkers is a standalone, full length, MFM ménage romance starring two huge, dominant warriors who make it all about the woman.

The buck stood grazing on the edge of the forest stream, its crown of proud antlers reflected in the rippling water. I watched hidden in the shadows. I'd tracked the buck for miles, loosening my muscles and enjoying the hunt, and I could almost taste my prey. A real wolf wouldn't be able to take down so large a quarry without its pack. A man could kill a buck with bow and arrow, and struggle to carry it back to his home. But I was neither human nor true wolf.

The wind shifted, and brought a flurry of scents. Among the usual bouquet, I smelled something sour. Another wolf, but not a familiar one. I knew the scents of my pack. This was an intruder.

The wind shifted and the buck grazed closer to my hiding place. My wolf forgot the worrying scent and focused on the prey immediately across the stream.

I Changed. In one instant the water below me reflected a man, with hard muscles and dark hair. Then an unnatural wind stirred the leaves, and in place of a man stood a great black wolf.

The buck raised its head at the unfamiliar wave of magic. It caught scent of the wolf I had become, and ran.

It was a short chase.

Afterward, licking the blood off my paw, I felt reluctant to change back. Men were slow and stupid, and bound by rules. They couldn't even smell the kaleidoscope of colors that the forest was, choosing instead to destroy everything with fire and live in smelly shacks in the mud.

Was not the world so much more beautiful as a wolf?

But beneath the simple, animal consciousness, lurked a darker beast. Even now, with the taste of blood in my mouth, the rage-filled creature struggled for dominance. I wrestled with it, shaking my wolf head as if worried by flies. My frantic inner fight brought me to the stream where I watched my canine features grow and Change into something grotesque...

My canine nose caught a pale scent, wafting all the way down from the mountain my pack called home. The smell told me a woman lived there. Not just any woman. Our woman.

Our mate.

The beast receded. Sanity returned.

I savored the woman's scent--light and cool, perfumed and perfect amid the sweaty stench of the warriors. She was waiting.

One more breath of her luscious scent, and I shifted. Paws became hands, fur became hair, and the bloodlust of the beast died as if it had never been.

I ran all the way home, carrying the buck.

At the top of the mountain path, a giant warrior stood guard, honing his axe. Wulfgar had been a deadly warrior even before becoming a Berserker. His blunt features brightened at the sight of fresh meat.

I slung the deer at his feet.

"Good hunt?" The massive warrior gave an appreciative sniff.

I grunted. After being a wolf, speech took its time returning.

Wulfgar barked an order to another wolf. "Roast the choicest bits over the fire for the Alpha's woman. Give the rest to the pack."

I nodded my thanks to Wulfgar, and the small red-headed wolf that came to collect the carcass.

"Beta," they both acknowledged me with a dip of their heads, taking care to avert their eyes from mine out of respect for my rank. Even though Wulgar stood a full head taller than me, I was slightly more dominant, if only because of my bond with the Alpha, Samuel.

A breeze swept along the face of the mountain, stirring the smoke of the fire and bringing the sweet aroma of a woman to me.

I left the fire and entered the cave, following the stone passageway to the quarters I shared with Samuel...and her.

As I walked down the hall, the sweet scent grew stronger. I paused in the doorway to our rooms. Inside Samuel lounged in wolf form, tawny streaks in his grey hide.

I nodded to him and headed straight for the pelt covered dais we used as a bed, to peek at the dark-haired woman burrowed in the furs.

Still asleep, Samuel spoke through our bond.

Best we stop wearing her out, I grinned at him.

He almost smiled. He'd been a Berserker so long, and spent almost a century half mad with magic. I'd been the tether holding him to the world, keeping him from a killing rage that would rape his mind. We'd fought Samuel's beast, together, and searched high and low for the woman the witch told us would save him—a woman marked by the wolf.

Brenna.

A deep breath, and the scent of her filled my lungs. The wolf quieted. I hadn't even realized how restless it was until I saw her, and relaxed. She smelled of moss and pine and the soft secret places in the forest that are safe.

No wonder our great Alpha basked at her feet in wolf form, his tongue lolling out like a puppy. After centuries of fighting, we'd finally found home.

I started to lie beside her on the dais and Samuel gave a half growl.

I won't wake her, I said through the bond. *Not just yet. I just want to lie close to her.*

I waited for his nod, then stretched out, tucking myself around her in the pelts.

Edging closer, I buried my face in her wealth of dark hair.

She stirred.

I bowed my body around her, letting her warmth seep into me, reveling in the soft curves of her body.

Beside the dais, Samuel watched in wolf form, panting happily.

My hand slipped between the pelts to cup her breast. I played with the soft handful, feeling her nipple harden and body come alive. I longed to hear her soft sigh of arousal, and a few seconds later, I was rewarded with the lovely sound.

We kept our beloved naked most of the time, furnishing her with a few dresses and wraps but mostly keeping the brazier burning around the room. Samuel and I lived in wary alert to protect our woman from any other. Even our pack, our warrior brothers, weren't to be trusted. Her scent was a siren call, too compelling and sweet. We kept her safe in this chamber, hidden from the world.

I closed my eyes and inhaled, giving the wolf what it craved, filling my lungs with the essence of her.

My body throbbed with need.

"Brenna," I breathed onto the back of her neck.

She sighed and everything in me focused on that slight sound. Her head tilted and her hair spilled off her neck, revealing the spidery scars at her throat, the scar evidence of a brutal wound she sustained as a child. The attack took her voice. It was a wonder it didn't take her life, but she survived.

Now she was ours.

Brenna shifted against me and my body responded, leaping to life, blood rushed to my groin. I grunted a little as I slipped an arm under her and tightened my hold on her, drawing her against my chest.

She wasn't a small woman by human standards, but compared to us, she was slight and perfect. Her softness made her all the more inviting.

Her bottom brushed my cock and I groaned into her hair.

Daegan, Samuel chided via the bond. *You woke her.*

"Couldnae be helped," I said out loud. "Such a bonny temptation."

My hand started exploring the softness of her breast, the smooth dip of her belly ending in the gently flaring hips.

"Wake up lass," I crooned in her ear as my fingers played south of her belly. "I'll make it worth yer while."

Her eyes fluttered open.

Not for the first time, I wished that our beloved could speak. The scars on her throat made her mute. Though she never had any trouble making her feelings known, I would give anything to hear her say my name.

My fingers searched for that wet sweet place between her legs, working to draw out a gasp. I smiled when I heard it leave her lips.

She sighed again and I wondered how awake she was. Then she shook her bottom against my groin. Her cheek curved with a smile and I knew she was awake.

"Naughty lass," I said, "getting me all worked up for ye." I propped myself on an elbow above her. "Don't ye know you're already enough of a temptation?"

She lay on her back, blinking up at me with those sultry, sleepy eyes.

I couldn't take it any longer; I leaned down and claimed her mouth. My fingers dipped and swirled between her legs, making her hips dance.

Magic pulsed through the room as Samuel made the Change from wolf to man. He took his place close to us.

Shifting over Brenna, I kissed my way down the slopes of her neck and breasts, not stopping until I tasted the secret place between her legs.

She tensed but I held her legs open, lapping at the pink center while she writhed.

At her head, Samuel captured our beloved's mouth, his hand at her breast. With fingers, lips and tongues, we worked our beloved's body until she vibrated between us like a lute's string, strummed to the point of breaking. Samuel let her mouth go and nibbled at her ear while I nibbled below. From her wild gasps and writhing, her body teetered on the edge of pleasure. We pinned her between us until she crested and shattered.

As she panted to catch her breath, Samuel and I shared a grin.

"Beautiful," he said so Brenna could hear.

"Aye." I nuzzled her inner thigh.

After a minute she blinked, raising her head. Without speaking, Samuel and I switched places. He pulled her to hands and knees and positioned himself behind her. She moved obediently as he propped her hips high and reached down to tease her folds.

I guided my beloved's head to my aching cock. She obeyed my silent command, sucking me so deeply my knees almost gave out.

"Och, lass." My hand stroked her cheek.

Samuel gripped her hips and I held Brenna's face still, preparing for his thrust. She gasped as he surged forward. The force of his movement drove her forward onto my own cock, and for a second I popped into her throat. The pressure took my breath away.

The bond between the Alpha and I hummed in harmony as we sawed our beloved's body between us. I cradled her face carefully as she rocked back and forth between us.

Samuel reached under again and stimulated her to another orgasm. Her gasps leaked around my cock and I came cursing, my hand fisted in her dark hair.

Pleasure poured down the bond between us, and Samuel's eyes glazed with lust. His canines flashed as he teetered on the brink between man and mindless beast.

I pulled out of my beloved's mouth with a pop, backing away at Samuel's signal. The giant blond warrior knelt naked behind our woman, his golden hair hanging about his shoulders. He smoothed a hand down Brenna's back, steadying her, readying her for a good fucking.

With a growl, he surged forward. His hips beat into her backside and a slapping sound filled the cavern. As Samuel kept up the brutal pace, Brenna's hands fisted into the pelts, her breath hitching in her broken throat.

"Cum." With the order, Samuel's palm smacked down on the side of her upturned ass. Brenna's eyes rolled back into her head as she obeyed, thrashing.

Samuel shuddered over her, large hands holding her hips up as he finished deep inside her. Once he pulled out, he took a handful of her hair and drew her to his cock, biding her clean it with her mouth. As I watched her lick submissively, my cock hardened again. The beast within craved dominance over our beloved, demanded her sweet submission. And it did not want to stop there...

I shut off that line of thought and flopped onto my side beside her, toying with her hanging breasts and admiring the flushed state of her skin.

"Lovely, lovely lass," I told her, and murmured the words I wished were true. "Ye were meant for us."

Much later I stood guard over our beloved while Samuel was gone. I watched her sleep, noting the fall of raven dark hair, the cheeks pale as moonlight.

Mine, said the wolf, and I wanted to agree. She was ours in every way we could make her. We'd bought her from her family a few moons ago, and kept her in our lair, away from the pack. She seemed to accept us. We brought her news of her remaining family--her three sisters thrived in the village. Two moons ago her mother died, we brought her the news. Samuel asked if she wanted to see the grave and Brenna shook her head no.

She'd left her old life, for us. And every time we claimed her, we felt we'd come home. But did she truly belong here?

She is ours. Samuel felt my uncertainty and spoke through the bond.

For as long as we keep her. I reminded him.

Why would we ever let her go?

I sent him the memory of hunting the buck earlier. *It happened again. I almost lost control of the beast.*

Silence. Samuel did not want to acknowledge that what we feared most might happen--the very beast Brenna soothed might rage again.

The Berserker rage was legendary on the battlefield. Many kings used it to gain power. In times of peace, the beast craved bloodshed. The magic that made us wolves carried a taint, and would drive us to madness. That was the price of our great power.

Brenna didn't know any of this. She didn't know several of the pack had succumbed to the beast and met their fate. When the beast took their mind, Samuel was waiting. More than a few had died, necks snapped and bodies flung off the mountain by the raging Alpha. Not because his control broke; because theirs did. Samuel protected the pack, even from its own members. But there was only so much he could do to keep the taint from spreading. We were warriors seasoned with many battles, but could not win the war for our minds. Before we'd consulted the witch to find Brenna, we were losing.

I remembered the nights when the beast howled for blood...

Tell me what happened, Samuel said finally. *How did you regain control?*

I caught our beloved's scent.

Just as the runes foretold. She soothes the beast.

I reached out and ran a finger over our beloved's smooth cheek. Her skin was so soft, so sweetly scented. Tonight she smelled like moonlight on the snow, and secrets kept deep in the earth...things no man had words for, things that only a wolf would understand.

My hand closed around her neck. Her pulse beat against my palm.

Both Samuel and I feared the day she'd wake and discover who we truly were. Not just werewolves, but Berserkers, cursed with tainted magic. We told Brenna not to fear the wolf, but never mentioned what she truly should fear: the beast.

She'd seen us in wolf form, but she hadn't seen the beast. Not even close.

Did she know when we took her, hard and fast, without thought, what monster lurked in our minds? Did she sense how much the beast wanted to hurt her?

My fingers closed over her throat. Once I had almost lost control. It could never happen again.

We cannot keep hiding the beast from her, Samuel's thought echoed across the bond. I snatched my hand away guiltily. *She will meet it, one way or another.*

Nay, it's too dangerous. This was why we'd spent centuries alone.

If she is to be our mate, she needs to meet the pack, learn our ways. We can't keep her inside forever.

But, I struggled to put my feelings into words. *What if she meets the beast, and can no longer love us?*

Can she truly love us, if she doesn't know what we are?

The beast does not love. It will try to destroy her.

I held my breath until Samuel answered, *Pray that it does not succeed.*

2

Restless, I left Brenna sleeping alone and went to find food. I stood at the mouth of the cave, blinking in the sunlight. Wulfgar crouched in man form beside the fire, roasting the meat.

"What news?" I asked.

"The Red Pack sends word. The full moon after next they gather for the Thing. They requested our emissary."

I frowned. "Odd request." There weren't many wolf packs on the island, and the one closest to us, the Red Moon Pack, regarded us as mortal enemies. The last time one of our pack encountered them, he'd been beaten and would've been killed, had Samuel not shown up in time.

It was the second time my Alpha had saved my life.

Wulfgar grunted. He knew the Red Pack hated us. "Hunters encroaching closer, and they want to do something about it."

"Meaning they want us to do something about it," I corrected. "Verrae well. Send word that I will attend."

I smelled his hesitation. "They want Samuel."

"They get me," I snarled. This time, my old pack wouldn't find me so easily bested.

Wulfgar bowed his head.

"Besides," I said in a lighter tone. "They dinnae call me Daegan Silvertongue for naught." I was more adept at the finesse of politics than our strong Alpha. Besides, someone had to remain on the mountain, with Brenna. She was a secret we could not afford to reveal.

Wulfgar's head dipped a little lower, even though he was a head taller than me and any other pack member, he took a deferential pose in respect of my dominance.

We waited for the meat to finish cooking. Most wolves ate their catch raw, but cooking meat satisfied the man, and allowed us to feel civilized again. Besides, we had to cook it for Brenna.

Berserkers lounged about the clearing, some as wolves and others in warrior form. Since Brenna's arrival, the pack was healthier, the bloodlust muted. The peace that flowed from our beloved to Samuel and I reached the pack through the Alpha bond.

I prayed the peace would last. The beast had been restless these past few days. One wrong word, or move, and it might break free, and everything we dreaded would come to pass. The beast loved breaking beautiful things.

To wash away my fear, I turned my thoughts to Brenna. My body stirred merely at the thought of her, her flawless skin and tempting curves, her shining hair spilling over the pelts. I could eat and drink of her day and night and never get enough.

I could almost smell her perfect scent even over the smoke and fire. I half closed my eyes and inhaled.

My eyes snapped open when I realized I wasn't imagining her scent. My beloved stood at the entrance of the cave, barefoot and clad in a simple shift we'd provided for her.

Her eyes widened as she took in the rocky clearing full of warriors and wolves.

"Brenna," I snapped, rising. Every wolf in the clearing swung his head towards her, their faces full of one dangerous emotion: desire.

Brenna sensed it. In an instant she did the worst thing she could've done. She took a step backwards. Retreat, and a wolf knows you're weak.

I launched myself across the clearing, but not before a young red haired warrior darted to her side. Fergus was the smallest of us, but he had the strength to lift a buck thrice his size and carry it up the mountain. He would break our beloved and not even realize he'd tried.

A second after I realized I would not reach Brenna in time, a hand came out of nowhere and clamped onto the youth's shoulder. "Change," Wulfgar ordered, and Fergus' body obeyed. The young man turned into wolf, following the command of the third most dominant in the pack. A few other warriors winced as the order blew through them like a cold wind, almost forcing their own Change.

I bowled past the two of them, grabbed Brenna and hoisted her over my shoulder.

"You're in trouble now, lass."

She squirmed and I backed up my words with a sharp swat on her backside as I strode down the cave hall to our rooms carved out of the mountain.

"We told ye not to leave our quarters, lass. What were ye thinking?" Real fear rose in me, and I pushed it down, turning to anger instead.

I heard a grunt behind me and I whirled, snarling. A

blond warrior had followed us, unable to resist the siren scent of our woman.

He growled a challenge.

"Mine," I snarled back. I shrugged Brenna off my shoulder and pushed her towards our quarters, at the same time stepping between her and the would-be attacker. "Back off, Siebold."

The warrior crouched in preparation to fight, a wild light in his gold eyes. His shoulders hunched as he roared in challenge.

"Change," I barked, and put the power of the Alpha behind it.

Siebold fell onto hands and knees, fur appearing along the ridge of his spine. His bones snapped and crackled as his wolf took over. "Stay." I ordered smugly, and left him in the hallway, howling in defeat.

I paused on the threshold and took a deep breath, fighting to control my feelings before I entered our room.

Brenna waited with arms crossed over her chest. She didn't look afraid. She looked incensed.

She met my gaze boldly, but when I prowled up to her she had the good sense to back away.

My hand went around her neck, collaring her. My skin burned when it touched the silver torc we'd given her to wear.

My own beast was close to breaking free.

I forced it back.

With effort, I removed my hand from around her throat. With both hands, I wrenched the torc open and removed it. I dangled the bent metal in front of her face.

"Ye agreed to wear this, aye?"

She nodded.

"Knowing what it would mean? Knowing that ye would have to live among the pack, and obey us?"

She nodded again. I threw the torc on the floor. She flinched as silver struck stone, but her eyes never left mine.

"You agreed to live among us, to obey Samuel and I and follow our rules? Rules that protect ye? Rules that keep ye safe?

Her forehead furrowed, but she still nodded. She knew where I was going and didn't like it.

"Ye are a woman of honor, Brenna, I knew it from the first. Were ye trying to leave? To go back on yer word?"

She shook her head.

"Ye broke a rule, Brenna. We left ye alone, but I was soon to return with food. We will never leave you alone for long. That is the reason Samuel and I claimed ye together. If one of us falls, the other will provide for ye." I dragged a frustrated hand through my hair. My wolf was howling for me to throw her to the floor and take her now, mark her with my seed, so she and any other wolf knew who she belonged to.

The beast also lurked, ready to pounce the minute I lost control. Like the wolf, it wanted to claim our beloved, but it also craved blood, and pain.

I dragged in a breath and tried to stay calm. "We care for ye. But we need ye to follow the rules. Understand?"

She nodded, the anger had left her face. She wasn't yet contrite, but close enough.

I pointed to the torc on the floor. "So choose again, Brenna. Will ye stay? Knowing ye must submit to our rules?" My heart quivered a little. She could say no. Was I really allowing her to choose again whether she would leave us? Would she return her to her family if she refused to pick up the torc? In my heart of hearts I knew I would. It would mean death for me and Samuel, and possibly the entire pack, but I would do it.

The knowledge should've frightened me. Instead, I felt stronger. "Do ye choose us?"

She nodded. Inside, I rejoiced, but kept my voice stern. Brenna could've died today, torn apart by wolves in rut. I had to make her understand.

"Then ye deliberately disobeyed us and must face the consequences." I pointed to the floor.

Uncertainty crossed her face.

I snapped my fingers in her face. "Submit. Now, lass. I'm not in the mood to be trifled with."

She stiffened, but she sank down.

At the sign of her submission, my anger receded.

"Pick up the torc."

She did so. Her usually graceful fingers trembled, but not with fear. With need. My eyes widened as I realized my dominance excited her. As I watched the pulse flutter in her throat, my own body quickened at the scent of her desire.

"Offer it to me." Instinct kicked in and she kept her eyes lowered as she offered up the circlet. I felt more powerful in this moment than in a lifetime of conquering others on the battlefield.

"Good lass." I accepted the torc and moved behind her, keeping my voice gentle. "Lift yer hair."

She obeyed and I felt my body tighten further at her submission. I replaced it around her slender neck.

"Rise, Brenna."

My hand cupped her neck again, pulling her close. "Look at me," I encouraged, and she did.

"Ye belong to us. Forever." My thumb played over her lips. Eyes on mine, she opened her mouth, and bit the tip of my finger.

My control snapped.

I pushed forward, half lifting her and carrying her to the nearest surface to rut. The dais was too far away, but I made it to the wall, pressing my beloved against the hard surface. Her head hit the stone but the lust in her face told me she didn't care. Her hands roved over my arms and shoulders. Her nails dug into the taut muscle as I held her aloft.

"Ye don't leave the cave without permission," I growled. She deserved punishment, but I was too angry to mete it out. I was too angry to do anything but fuck her.

She glared at me and tugged at my shoulders, pressing her lower half closer to mine. My hands found the top of her shift and rent it in two, baring her body to me. The desire to bite into her shoulder, to make her bleed, to hold her by the scruff of the neck and shake her was almost overpowering. But she wasn't a female wolf who could handle such rough punishment. I would have to settle for fucking our naughty human against the wall, hard.

I hitched one leg up around my hip and thrust inside her.

Her whole body rocked backwards. Her mouth opened in a perfect circle of satisfaction.

I drove into her again and again, steadying her so her head didn't slam against the wall, but otherwise not holding back. She gripped my forearms and tilted her hips, accepting the punishing thrusts, welcoming them.

"I can barely control myself around ye," I told her. "You think the pack will hold back? You'd be lucky to survive."

My hand collared her neck, pressing into the torc, feeling the reassuring coolness of the silver against my palm. She could've died today at the hands of the pack. The beast within didn't know love or gentleness. Even now, I wanted to whip and fuck her into submission.

I'd settle on the latter until I was under control.

I let go of her neck and braced one hand against the wall. The other cradled her head while my hips snapped forward. "Ye will remember who owns you. We are yer masters. And ye will obey us so ye do not come to harm."

She panted in my ear.

She was enjoying it. Good. I wasn't going to stop until I'd marked her with my seed. I couldn't go outside and tear out the eyes of every wolf that'd beheld her, but I could mark her as mine.

I lifted her slightly, driving up into her, trying to plant myself so deep inside her body she'd feel me forever. As I groaned her name, she angled her head and kissed my neck.

The tender act sent a shudder through my body. "Och, lass."

Her body tightened and she started to convulse. As her orgasm took her, her knees buckled and she sagged against me. Holding her close, I ground into her hips, letting my own pleasure wash over me.

We stayed close like that, my body pinning hers to the wall.

I felt Samuel enter the room before he spoke.

"What's going on?"

I stepped back, letting her feet touch the ground again.

"I'm teaching our beloved a lesson." I felt a lot better as I ran my hands down her naked form. Brenna shot a sorrowing look at her torn shift on the floor. We rarely allowed her any clothes, thinking that keeping her naked would reinforce our orders to stay in our quarters, away from the pack. We were right. She'd have to earn the right to clothes again, along with our trust.

Samuel folded his massive arms over his chest. "Wulfgar is out there with Fergus at his feet in wolf form. Siebold is in such a state I sent him to the northern watch. It seems our Brenna caused quite a stir."

"She left the cave, put herself in danger."

"Is this true?" Samuel snapped, golden eyes heating as he glared at Brenna.

Our woman nodded, her gaze on the ground. At least she was smart enough not to goad an angry Alpha.

"'Tis partly my fault," I offered. "I left her alone for too long."

"That shouldn't matter," Samuel said, and spoke to me over the bond. We can't keep her in the cave forever.

It's too dangerous, I protested.

I don't like it either, but if she's to remain with us, she needs to learn our ways. It is time.

Samuel held out his hand. "Brenna."

Slowly she left my side and walked to the Alpha. I folded my arms to hide my nervousness. At least I could enjoy the sight of my seed trickling down her thigh.

Our Brenna wasn't a small woman, but Samuel's great body dwarfed hers. Her head only came up to his chest. As she approached, Samuel schooled his features into a benign expression. He had the advantage of size and strength, he took care not to intimidate her.

Samuel sat on the dais and drew our beloved closer to stand between his legs. For a minute he only toyed with her hair, pushing it off her bare shoulders.

"I'm going to tell you the rules. You already know one— do not leave the quarters without our permission. You broke that rule, and in a moment I'll have Daegan punish you."

Brenna glanced at me with wide eyes and I winked back. After spending myself deep inside her, my wolf felt calmer. The beast was satisfied. My calm wouldn't stop me from spanking my beloved's bottom bright red, but instead of losing control, I'd enjoy the act.

She wouldn't be able to say the same.

Samuel gripped her shoulders as he thought of how to explain our ways to our little human. I didn't envy him.

"You must understand the wolfpack runs on careful hierarchy. Daegan and I are at the top. As Alpha, I lead the pack, but I also serve it. If an enemy attacks, I am the first to fight. If the enemy succeeds, I am the first to die. In return, the pack gives me respect. I eat first, I have first right to any luxury. Most importantly, if I give an order, the pack must obey."

I circled the room, replenishing the wood in the braziers. In the pack, I was called "Daegan Silvertongue" for my ability to speak circles around most wolves, but as Alpha, Samuel had the final say. We agreed it was best for him to instruct the new pack members in the rules. When a wolf broke the rules, Samuel judged and ordered punishment.

"You are not a wolf, but you are now a member of the pack. As a human you are...weak. Frail. Unable to protect yourself. I protect any weak wolf in the pack from death, as long as they keep to their place. But I cannot step in all the time. Wolves naturally fight for their place in their pack. It is not my responsibility to stop a stronger wolf from fighting a weaker one, if the weaker wolf challenged him for dominance. Do you understand what I've said so far?"

He waited for Brenna's slow nod.

"Like it or not, you are the weakest in the pack. We will protect you, but if you leave our quarters and walk among the wolves, you are subjected to the rules. You must never look another wolf in the eyes, whether he is in wolf or man form. Doing so means you've challenged that wolf for dominance, and you must fight to uphold your claim. They will fight you to keep their place in the pack. That is not a fight you would win."

"If I hadnae stepped in, Fergus or another would've either challenged ye or tried to claim ye. Either way, blood would've been shed. Do ye ken?"

Her gaze darted between us and Samuel caught her chin. "It is very dangerous to challenge a wolf. More than a few seconds of eye contact is a declaration of dominance."

"Ye cannae look another wolf in the eye, unless ye are willing to fight him. The only one who can look any other wolf in the eyes is Samuel. Even I cannae face him as an equal."

"Daegan is almost as dominant as I am. His strength is matched with his leadership and cunning. Long ago our wolves decided to rule together. We are linked as warrior brothers, pledged to keep the pack safe, even if one of us falls in battle, the other will succeed him. That is why we share you without fighting. But even he must defer to me." My Alpha raised his voice. "Daegan look at me."

I met his golden eyes as ordered, but after a few seconds my wolf protested, and I pulled my gaze away to meet Brenna's brown ones.

"Ye see, lass? We all must abide by the rules for the good of the pack."

"The next time you step out of this cave without permission, and face a wolf on your own, you will be punished," Samuel said.

Brenna sighed and nodded.

"You're lucky I was close, today. Fergus is the youngest among us and the quickest to lose control. I do not know what he'd do if he'd caught ye—fought or fucked ye. But it wouldnae end well." I felt a tinge of fear, thinking about what could've happened if Fergus had reached Brenna before Wulfgar stopped him.

"Fergus will be disciplined and shamed in front of the entire pack. But we cannot allow you to go unpunished for breaking our rule and leaving the cave. You knew this rule."

"I ken it's difficult to stay inside, Brenna," I said. "But it's for yer protection."

"In time you will accompany us outside," Samuel allowed.

"Samuel will allow you to walk among the pack. But ye must heed his words, and keep yer eyes lowered."

"Submit, Brenna," Samuel said, almost pleading. "It is not an easy thing we ask, but it is necessary. Will you obey?"

Eyes downcast, she nodded.

He lifted her chin. "There is an exception to the rule. Unless we specifically desire your submission, you may always meet our gaze. The wolf wants you to act as our mate. So you, Brenna," he smiled, "are the only member of the pack my wolf will allow to meet my gaze. Do you see why you are so precious to me?"

He kissed her, and I felt his feelings through the bond. Not just pleasure. Relief.

"You are a gift we did not deserve. We cannot see you harmed." His finger played over her lips, before he sat back. "That is why you must obey us, completely. You left the cave without permission. Daegan left while you were sleeping to get you food. If you cannot obey a rule for a few minutes, we will chain you to the bed."

"I wouldnae mind tying ye down." I winked.

Samuel rolled his eyes. "Daegan takes delight in subduing unwilling victims. He also will enjoy disciplining you."

"One of us should." I extended a hand "It's time, lass. Come."

As soon as Brenna came within arm's length, I pulled her over my knees.

I held her off balance, her fingers brushing the floor, Her pale buttocks propped high. My sweet woman writhed on my lap, massaging my cock until I pinned her and steadied her with a leg over hers.

"None of that, now. Take yer punishment like a good lass." I couldn't keep the joy out of my tone.

Spanking one cheek then the other, smacking the pert flesh. I took care not to use even half my strength, but after a minute a blush spread over her arse.

Samuel watched from a healthy distance. His wolf was too dominant for it to be safe for him to punish her. He would not be able to keep control. Besides, he didn't really enjoy punishing beautiful women, not like I did.

Part of me was really worried. Our woman couldn't go about challenging the pack. They'd either claim and fuck her, or fight her for dominance, killing her in the process.

I spanked until I heard a gasp. When I stopped and righted her, the stubborn tilt of her mouth had softened. One small tear fell and I brushed it away. From the looks of her, spanking had set her firmly in a state of submission.

"Up now and go to the wall. Nose to the stone and wait there for a few minutes." I rubbed her bottom to relieve some of the pain, then sent her off with a playful swat. "No touching yer arse, unless ye want another session over my lap."

She hesitated, but did as I asked. Her face burned with humiliation, but she still didn't look repentant. I sighed. I didn't want to beat out her spirit, but we'd have to keep an eye on her. We might not be so lucky the next time she broke the rules.

After a few minutes, the sound of heavy footsteps echoed in the corridor. Wulfgar paused in the doorway to request entry, and waited until Samuel allow it.

"Alpha," Wulfgar rumbled respectfully.

Brenna stiffened and started to turn around.

"Eyes to the wall, lass," I said to Brenna. "This is part of the punishment." Her body stiffened and I leaned and spoke soothingly. "Tis only one of our soldiers, come to see that we upheld the laws of the pack. We will not let him harm ye."

"Wulfgar," Samuel greeted the visiting warrior. The two had fought many battles together, since the witch changed them both to Berserkers.

"There she is," the Alpha continued, inviting the warrior to look at the woman standing in disgrace like a naughty child. My wolf didn't like exposing our beloved like this, but Samuel had to follow protocol. "You see she has been punished."

Wulfgar nodded. For all his great mass, he was the most in control of all the wolves. Not quite as dominant as Samuel, but certainly strong enough to challenge for Alpha, if he wanted it.

The Viking's eyes, when not gold with magic, were grey. They swept over Brenna's naked form, heating only for a second before he politely averted his gaze and nodded to Samuel. He would report to the pack that justice had been done, punishment delivered.

"She is new. She will learn," Samuel said.

The giant nodded again.

"How is Fergus?"

"I'll keep him in wolf form a few days," Wulfgar grunted. "Cool him down." Custom called for the injured party—

poor Fergus—come to inspect the wrongdoer and see that punishment was meted out, but Wulfgar had come in the more unstable wolf's stead. Most pack discipline was carried out in public, but we would not stand for our beloved to be put on display in front of all of the Berserkers. Not unless it was necessary.

"Will the pack be satisfied?" Samuel asked.

Wulfgar nodded. "I'll carry word to them that justice was done."

"Thank you, Wulfgar." Samuel said.

Another nod of the shaven head, and Wulfgar left.

I leaned against the wall, running my hand down Brenna's back when I noted her trembling.

"It's alright, lass. He's gone."

She blinked hard, forcing back tears of anger or embarrassment.

I took her into my arms, holding her stiff body close, tipping her head back and brushing away one tear that escaped down her cheek. "None of that now. We would not let ye come to harm."

I paused, silently asking Samuel to help me explain.

"We bent the rules by disciplining you in private. Fergus is not so lucky. The whole pack knows he is forced to stay in wolf form for a few days, as punishment for nearly attacking you. Wulfgar will carry the tale of your punishment back to the rest of the warriors. Otherwise they would come and demand to see evidence of your discipline themselves."

"We cannae abide that." I shuddered. Brenna shot me a furious look as if to say "It must be so difficult for you." She wrenched away from me. Her red bottom jiggled enticingly as she strode to the dais and picked out a pelt to cover her naked form. Her chin stayed in the air, as haughty as a queen's.

I bit back a smile. The punishment had bruised her pride, but not broken her. As bright as her bottom was now, the marks would fade quickly. We had to make sure the lesson stayed.

"Brenna," Samuel called. "Come here." Our beloved avoided my eyes as she marched to where he sat. The big blond set her on his knee. She winced as her punished behind hit his hard muscled thigh, but gritted her teeth.

"You're a brave girl to take your punishment so well. I know you are new here but you must understand. Any wolf who harms you will be put to death. If Daegan had not interfered...We do not wish to see you hurt.

She glared at Samuel as if to say, *Then why am I sitting on a red arse?*

"You live among us now. Wolf packs thrive best when there's a series of rules." Samuel spoke quietly but firmly. "You must abide by the rules, or next time, I'm afraid, your punishment must be public." He ran a finger over the silver circlet at her neck.

"This torc claims you as ours, but it is small protection against a raging warrior."

"We were lucky today," I spoke up. "Fergus is the smallest of us, and weak. But if ye had challenged a more dominant wolf..."

Samuel shuddered, real fear on his face. "Please, please do not test our control," he pleaded. Brenna blinked as if shocked the Alpha would beg so humbly. "Please, Brenna. We cannot lose you. Do you see why Daegan had to punish you?"

Brenna gave a short nod.

"Daegan enjoys meting out punishment, but he will make it up to you." Samuel glanced my way. "Won't you?"

"Oh aye," I said glibly. I seated myself on a stone close to the dais, a jar of salve in hand. "Come lie over my lap."

Brenna raised an eyebrow and I grinned at her.

"Ye don't trust me, lass?"

Samuel pushed her towards me. I enjoyed the sight of her bare body sashaying back towards me. When she draped herself over my knees, my cock hardened further, I gave a contented sigh.

"I could sit like this all day," I joked. I stroked a hand down her back, and she shivered. "Ye did so well taking yer punishment. Let me give ye a little reward."

Scooping out a generous handful of salve, I rubbed it into her reddened bottom. The spanking's sting would already be fading, leaving a warm glow behind.

Brenna squirmed a little and I caught a whiff of her sweet musk. The heady scent told me just how much the spanking affected her. Perhaps this was the source of her humiliation.

I let my fingers wander lower, slipping between her legs to check.

"Just as I suspected. Soaked."

Samuel chuckled.

Brenna started to rise up and I held her down.

"No, no, no lass, let me see to ye. Tis only fair after I caused ye pain." I kept her pinned as I swirled my salve covered fingers over her sweet lower lips. She squirmed in earnest, giving my cock its own lovely massage.

It was a fun game.

Finally I let her up and she backed away, her face as red as her bottom. I raised my fingers to my mouth and slurped at my juice covered digits.

Brenna frowned and I winked at her.

Samuel caught her, pulling her back flush to his front.

His big body dwarfed her. He wore a loin cloth and quickly pulled it off, rubbing his cock into her hot rear.

"Did you like how Daegan made it up to you?"

His hands roved over our beloved's bare form. She struggled but her eyes glazed and her mouth fell open, panting a little as he tugged at her nipples and reached down further to stroke his fingers over the tiny pleasure spot between her legs.

Her knees buckled and Samuel held her up as she sagged against him. He continued growling softly in her ear.

"Anytime you cross us, Daegan will spank your bottom. But I promise we'll take care of you. You're ours now."

He held her up with a burly arm under her breast. Her nipples stood out hard and pink, ready for a hot mouth to suck on them. My mouth watered.

"You're not afraid of us are you, little love? We would never truly hurt you."

I approached, fisting my cock. Bending my head to her breasts, I worried the little nubs, alternately sucking and licking and catching them between my teeth.

"A little spanking never hurt anyone," Samuel went on. "And you were such a good girl. We'll give you a reward."

His hand worked faster between her legs and she stiffened, mouth parted, eyes almost rolling back in her head.

"Come, Brenna," Samuel ordered.

I watched her body stiffen. Little gasps escaped her lips and I drew her forward into a searing kiss. "Pain and pleasure, lass," I breathed against her mouth. "But only at our hands, and ours alone."

"Ours alone," Samuel echoed softly, still holding her up. "Did you like that?" He nuzzled her ear as she blinked and recovered. "Are you ready to thank Daegan for correcting you?"

"Give us a kiss, lass." I stepped back, stroking my cock.

Samuel held her hips as she bent towards me. I stepped back and guided her lower.

"Not on my mouth...there's a good lass." My cock speared her mouth and she sucked obediently, still in a submissive haze.

Samuel lined up behind her and eased inside. We held her up as we scythed in and out, me at the fore and Samuel behind

He pistoned his hips hard, driving her onto my cock. I kept my hand gentle in her hair.

She held on to my side.

The bond hummed as Samuel and I moved in perfect sync.

My thumb brushed her cheek.

"So perfect for us."

Samuel reached down to swipe at her pleasure spot and she sighed over my member.

"Gods," I cried out, my own knees weakening. Vibrations moved up my entire body. Muscles tightening with pleasure, I came so hard I saw stars.

Samuel grunted as he sped up his thrust.

I helped lower Brenna to the floor and Samuel went to one knee, body bent over her.

As soon as I laid a pelt under her body, Samuel picked up her legs so he could drive as deep as possible. He held her easily. Her body flushed as pleasure rolled over her.

Samuel cursed in his old language as he finished. Below him, Brenna's body still trembled.

I rolled her in the pelt and carried her to the dais, laying her pale body out like a sacrifice to dark gods.

Samuel came to his feet, already recovered. We didn't

take our eyes off the woman before us. Blood roared through our bodies, hardening and making us ready.

Samuel stepped forward. "Again."

Behind us, someone started clapping. "What a thrilling performance," a cool voice wafted over the three of us.

I scrambled to my feet, snarling, and faced the tall, blonde woman standing at the entrance. A mocking smile curved her mouth. I'd been so taken by my thoughts I hadn't scented her approach. One sniff and I realized she had camouflaged her scent somehow. She smelled as bland and flat as the stone wall behind her.

"Witch, what are you doing here?" Samuel growled behind me, a powerful sound, tinged with magic. He stood at the foot of the dais, blocking our beloved from the witch's view. Beyond him, Brenna lay blinking, her face still soft from the pleasure we'd given her. Her hands grasped at the pelts, pulling them over her nakedness.

A growl sounded deep in my belly at having such a private moment disturbed by the unwanted guest.

"Ye tempt danger, Yseult, coming here uninvited," I said. "Best ye leave while we're in a good mood."

Samuel was less diplomatic. "Get out."

Yseult's eyes flashed, and I felt anger recede a little, beaten back by worry. Yes, she'd interrupted and shattered a beautiful moment. But the blonde witch was dangerous. She'd never been our true enemy, but we could not control her. If roused, she would be a formidable foe. I reached out to Samuel on our shared path, and our wolves snarled with shared sentiment.

We didn't want this woman around Brenna.

"If you don't want to be interrupted then why are you playing in an open cave in the middle of the day? Anyone could walk in and join you." The witch's voice was as cool and emotionless as her scent, making it damned hard to read her true feelings.

"The pack knows to stay away," I said, stepping forward, keeping my body in the line of sight between her and Brenna.

Yseult pretended to sniff. "I can smell her heat halfway down the mountain."

"You dare-" Samuel's rage choked him. I felt his grasp slip on the beast.

Samuel, no. I threw my energy down the bond, trying to hold back the tide of Berserker rage. As much as I wanted the witch out of our sanctuary, a wolf on the rampage would spell disaster. Not to mention as Alpha, he was likely to pull the entire pack into a bloody rampage.

Yseult wouldn't survive. But Brenna and most of the pack might not, either.

Samuel transferred his anger to me, and I staggered back, fighting to stay upright. The beast didn't want to be placated or stopped. I heard nothing, saw nothing, felt nothing but blind outrage. My world focused to a single intent: savage the witch. In my mind's eye she was already dead and bloodied on the floor.

And if we eat her, we absorb her power.

Magic rolled over me, and my knees started to buckle: a natural submissive reaction to my Alpha's anger. Pain blossomed in my skull: the brother bond opened me up to compulsion, but at least I would buffer it for the rest of the pack.

Why isn't she dead yet? The beast raged...no longer a wolf, but a mad thing, tainted by magic.

"Please," I choked.

Beyond Samuel, Brenna now sat upright, her face alert and expression worried.

As Samuel started to move forward, ready to hurt the witch, or me, or both, Brenna leaned forward and caught his hand.

"No, Brenna," I gasped, tearing my body off the floor in a desperate attempt to stand between her and the Alpha on the brink of losing control. Samuel could not hurt her.

Before I reached him, Samuel whirled towards Brenna, teeth bared His arm already looked shaggier with the impending Change.

His eyes fell on our beloved, calm and innocent in her cocoon of pelts.

The beast quieted.

I wouldn't have believed it if I hadn't witnessed it. Part of me wanted to glance at Yseult, to see if her mouth fell open at the sight of the raging Alpha, calmed with one woman's touch, like a sea storm blown away by a summer breeze.

Brenna smiled...and the sun came out.

Samuel smiled back, fully man, his wolf calm and sedate as a pup with its mother.

Yseult cleared her throat.

I had almost forgotten she was there.

The witch also smiled, but she looked uneasy, as if she'd seen something she didn't quite understand. "You did take my advice. And I see the results were satisfactory."

Her gaze flicked between us, and my wolf still felt uneasy, hating the smug look on her face.

Brenna's brow furrowed.

"It's alright, lass," I heard myself say. "It's only the witch —the one that led us to you."

Brenna's face went carefully blank. I felt a twinge of guilt. We'd approached her stepfather, paid him to lure her away from her family, and sell her to us. It wasn't the way I'd wished to meet the woman who would be our salvation, but it was fast. And Brenna had settled into her role.

At least, it seemed she had. I studied her guarded expression, wishing we could speak to her. Ask her what she thought of being consort to two Alphas. Whether our care for her would be enough to please her.

Back at the dais, Samuel helped our beloved rise and hovered over her while she tugged on a gunna. Yseult smirked at the sight of the burly warrior acting as a lady's maid, but Samuel ignored her, focusing on our beloved, taking care to stay calm after coming so close to losing his hold on the beast.

I turned my attention to the witch who'd stirred up so much trouble in the few minutes she was here. "What do you want, Yseult?"

"Merely to check on you. The last I saw you were hanging on, one claw away from descending into Berserker rage forever. The runes I cast gave me a glimpse into your possible future—and it was dark. But for the woman, of course. I'd wondered if you found her."

"We did." Samuel grunted. His tone made it clear that he wanted the woman to leave.

"Found and mated, I see." Yseult cocked her head, studying us as if we were particularly ugly insects crawling on her boots.

"Humans can't mate with wolves." I said automatically. It was true. Only a woman with some magic—part witch—could bear a werechild. My mother had been one of them. There were female weres but few and far between, and most would not mate with a Berserker wolf, tainted as we were with dark magic.

"Perhaps. Perhaps not."

"What do you speak of?" Samuel was losing patience. The big man crossed his arms over his chest.

"Funny, I sensed her heat. How often is she fertile? Every full moon? Have you not noticed how much stronger her scent is at that time? Both her scent and her...hunger."

"That is natural," Samuel bit off. In the few months Brenna had been with us, we'd noticed her intense need for us every full moon. "Human or wolf, every woman goes through that."

Yseult raised her eyebrows in silent challenge to his statement.

Brenna's cheeks were pink, but I could not spare her embarrassment. I had to know.

"Are you saying it is not natural for a human woman? Is Brenna going into heat, like a female of our kind?"

Yseult gave her damned enigmatic smile.

"Why don't you ask her? See what she says?"

Brenna sucked in a harsh breath. Her hand flew to her throat, covering the white weal across her neck.

"Oh yes," Yseult purred. "She is mute. I remember now."

Frowning at the witch's inconsiderate words, I went to stand by her. Samuel already tucked her to his front, arms around her in comfort

The witch watched us. This whole thing—interrupting our lovemaking, provoking Samuel, was a game. The wolf and man disliked being treated as a pawn.

"You knew this, damn you," I said in a frosty tone. "You were the first to find her."

Yseult raised her hands in defense. "Calm, Daegan, I merely read the runes. I never met the girl. I'm glad she suits."

"She suits," I agreed bluntly, and turned to look at

Brenna. My face softened. *She more than suits,* I spoke to Samuel through the bond, and he agreed.

Yseult looked annoyed. She knew wolves could speak to one another, and hated it. She liked to be the one who held the secrets.

"Tell us what you know," I ordered, without much hope that she would.

"My dear Daegan, I know nothing." She shrugged. "If you'd let me alone with her for a few moments—"

"No," Samuel growled.

"I might study the mark of the wolf," the witch went on coolly as if she hadn't been interrupted. "That is how you knew she was the one the runes spoke of, is it not? The wolf attack when she was young."

"Dog attack," I glared. "Her family told us it was a wild dog."

"Dog, wolf..." Yseult shrugged.

Samuel and I exchanged glances. Was it possible our Brenna had been mauled by another werewolf? And not just any sort of wolf, a creature like us, tainted with magic--a Berserker in the grip of madness?

Yseult's eyes gleamed. "Yes, you begin to see now. Did you ever ask yourself how she survived such a brutal attack? Did you ever wonder why?"

Samuel and I blinked, and looked to Brenna, who seemed just as confused as we were.

"Are you saying the reason she was attacked...and the reason she survived...there's a connection?"

Yseult's smile broadened.

"You speak in circles, witch. Either tell us, or leave."

"I will tell you, when I know for sure. But I want a favor in return."

"Favor?"

"The usual."

Samuel waved a hand. "The pack will fulfill the terms. Daegan and I will no longer take part."

"So faithful to this woman already? I never thought I'd live to see the day a woman tied you to her."

Samuel ignored the witch's jibe. "The pack will see to your needs."

"They are not also faithful to your Brenna? Or do you not share her?"

"Nay," I growled. "We will never share her."

"Pity," Yseult sniffed. "When the time comes to collect my favor, I should love to have another to help me...entertain the pack. Your wolves are so voracious...especially the scarred blond—what is his name?"

"Siebold," Samuel and I answered together. The large Viking had a sadistic streak that matched Yseult's blood craving. Of course she would favor him.

"Siebold, yes," Yseult purred. "I should love more time with him. Perhaps I could take him with me..."

"No," I said. Knowing the witch, she'd probably ask Siebold directly, and he might take her up on the challenge, so I added, "We would not allow him to go."

"Pity." Yseult didn't look too put out. "I shall have to wait until solstice, then." She smiled at me, probably recalling the last solstice, when Samuel and I took her together, while the pack watched.

Sure enough, an image appeared in my mind unbidden—the witch's body naked and writhing under me. The memory felt cold compared with the time I'd just spent with Brenna, even though it was the same act. There was no love between Yseult and I.

I turned away, wondering at the warm feelings I had for the dark-haired woman on the dais. Was it love?

"Our woman is hungry," Samuel said to Yseult. "You may take your leave."

"As you wish," Yseult said in a sour tone. We hadn't insulted her outright, but only just. The witch deserved it, even if it wasn't wise to anger a powerful one.

"One last thing," she said, and I tensed for her parting shot. "You've claimed this woman as your beloved, your true mate?"

I jolted at the use of "beloved"...the private name I had for Brenna. I wondered if it was possible the witch had plucked it from my thoughts.

"She is ours."

"Is she, truly? I only ask because I did not see a claiming mark."

Samuel placed his hand on Brenna's shoulder, where a werewolf would bite his mate during a breeding frenzy. "Human flesh is frail. She is ours, even if we do not mark her."

"Hmmm. How can you be sure, then, that she is your true mate?" Yseult held up three fingers. "Mating heat, mating bond, mating bite. Those are the signs of a were-wolf's true mate."

"What would you know of it?" Samuel demanded. Brenna couldn't bond with us, and couldn't survive a mating bite. She wasn't a werewolf, wasn't the proper candidate for a Berserker mate. But up until now, no woman had been. Yseult seemed to be testing our loyalty to our beloved, demanding proof of our love. Samuel looked frustrated. "Why do you care so much, unless you are jealous?"

Yseult turned pale, but retorted in a biting tone, "I only wish to serve, Alpha. You approached me to find the one who would bring your peace. If she is not the one--"

"She is the one." Samuel wrapped his arms around

Brenna, his giant hand palming her throat and covering the silver torc she wore for us.

"Then claim her."

Samuel released Brenna and set her carefully aside. I sensed my Alpha was close to losing his temper again, and this time, no calming touch of our woman would stop him.

"Yseult, perhaps it is time for ye to leave--"

Yseult followed me, but whirled at the last second. "If you do not form a mating bond, there are other wolves who would love to take her."

"Out!" Roared Samuel, his back already hunched with a half change...not into wolf but into a beast halfway between animal and man.

Yseult's face paled a little, and she stepped back, turning it into a mocking curtsy at the last.

"Until solstice."

EARS STILL RINGING with Samuel's anger, I let Yseult go ahead of me, and followed her away from our sleeping chamber. She strode through the stone hall with her chin in the air, revealing no sign that she had been cast out.

"Yseult," I called and she paused, keeping her stiff back to me. "Tell me, is it possible for a human to mate with a wolf?"

"A human? Pure? With all the magic stripped from them by their White Christ? No." Her tone mocked.

"So Brenna cannot be our true mate." Even as I stated it, the wolf inside me disagreed. *She is ours,* the wolf insisted. *Our true mate.*

I forced myself to meet Yseult's gaze. The witch seemed

to sense the wolf's disagreement, and my despair. The expression on her face was kin to pity.

"I will tell you, Daegan. I cast the runes before I came here."

"And?"

"You and Samuel must find your true mate before the next red moon or the beast will consume you."

I swallowed. I didn't know what that meant, and did not ask. It was possible Yseult herself didn't understand. If she did, she'd tell us when she was ready, not a moment before.

"I thought that Brenna would stop the madness."

"The runes fell as they would, Daegan." Yseult said in a sharp tone.

I searched her face. We'd been lovers once. Surely I could find some hint in her face as to what she felt.

Nothing.

I tried to reason with her. "You can see as well as I do... she soothes the beast."

"I am sorry," she said. "But as I tried to tell Samuel, there are three requirements."

I nodded. Mating heat, mating bond, mating bite.

"If you cannot accomplish those three things," she shrugged. "She is not your true mate."

"But the wolf claims her as mate."

"What of the beast? The third, darkest part of you—does the beast accept her?"

I shook my head.

How does a man feel when he suffers a mortal wound, and survives only to be told he will be hung on the morrow? I swallowed.

"Then what of Brenna?"

"Her presence is helpful, I suppose. But unless the beast sees her as a true mate..." Yseult shrugged. "You ask me what will become of her? What happens when the beast takes control? To anyone around you, be they villagers, loved ones, or even armies."

She would not have to look into my thoughts to see memories of the killing fields. They were written across my face, in the scars of my body, and regret in my gaze. "They die."

She nodded.

Every muscle in my body tightened.

If Brenna was not our true mate, when the beast finally did consume us, she would not survive.

An image flashed through my mind: a woman torn to pieces. Nothing left but a stain on the ground.

I tasted blood in my mouth, and almost vomited.

My insides twisted as I realized what Yseult was saying: if we loved Brenna we would send her away.

"How long do we have?" I rasped.

"As long as it takes for you to succumb to the madness. You may have a moon. You may have a day. Or perhaps it will take a century."

"She will not live for a century. Humans do not live that long."

"Then you best find your true mate soon."

"Is that why you came today? To warn us?"

"Yes. Believe it or not, I am a friend."

I didn't believe it. She was an ally, never a friend. If she revealed information now, it was because it suited her purposes.

Still, I thanked her gruffly.

She returned with a smile that did not quite reach her eyes. Her hips swayed as she walked away, a sight meant to entice. It made me feel sick.

Ye heard?

Aye, Samuel spoke through the bond.

We have to tell Brenna. She should know.

Silence.

Yseult paused at the mouth of the cave, and I strode to catch up with her, unwilling to let her linger among the pack.

"I'll see you to the path."

She nodded politely. If she sensed my distress, she said nothing.

Samuel?

We'll tell her.

The nausea in my stomach spread through my body. The wolf wanted to race after the witch, jaws snapping, and drive her from the mountain for bearing this news. It did not understand the future, or the choice before us.

It understood now and pain. And it wanted to retaliate.

For a moment my vision blurred with the desire to kill something. I waited until it cleared, and ambled out to the bonfire. Yseult strutted past the watching wolves, a few in man form.

"Hello, Siebold," she purred as she passed the warrior. The big blond sat bare-chested on a rock near the fire, sharpening his sword. He turned to watch her go.

"Siebold," I called, and after a long look at the disappearing woman, he gave me his attention. "Ye are on watch until dusk."

Anger crossed the man's face. He belonged to the group of warriors turned with Samuel in Northvegr to fight for a king called Harald Fairhair, long ago, before even I was born. I was only a pup when they came a-Viking from the cold lands, sailing here on dragon headed ships. For a seasoned warrior like Siebold, submitting to someone younger and less experienced must rankle the big warrior. I was more dominant, if only because of my link with Samuel. The Alpha trusted me.

Neither of us trusted Siebold.

"What did the witch want?"

"Ye," I couldn't resist teasing. "Trussed on a frame for her to fuck, then eat. We told her no."

Siebold snorted.

"You jest, Beta," he said in the sour tone I'd heard Yseult use. Maybe I could convince Samuel to hand the belligerent wolf over to the witch for her dark purposes.

"Don't pout, Viking," I called him by his nickname. "She'll be back midsummer for her pound of flesh, and her pounding." I winked at him. "Now trot up to yer post. I'll send relief at sundown."

Provoked, he snarled, human lips peeling back from teeth slightly sharper than a regular man's. Dropping the teasing act, I answered in kind. Teeth bared, I held his eyes, letting the wolf show a little until he dropped his gaze in respect for my dominance. Gripping his weapon, he rose and stalked up the mountain path to an overlook we used to keep watch.

Crouching by the fire, I used a dagger to poke at the roasting meat, alternately eating and setting aside slices for Brenna's meal.

I was about to leave when a shout stopped me.

"Beta," Wulfgar prowled across the clearing towards me, worry crossing his blunt expression. "A word. We had a visitor."

"Hunters?" We were half a day's run from the nearest village, but travelers sometimes strayed onto what we considered our lands.

"No. One of us."

Anger flooded through me. "Werewolf?" I snarled.

There was another pack close by, the Red Moon pack. We'd fought them years ago, establishing our right to the mountain. Perhaps it was time to revisit them, remind them of our claim.

"Yes, the scent belonged to a werewolf," Wulfgar continued cautiously. "But he did not smell natural born."

Hackles raised, I snapped. "Not Red Moon pack. Not unless they've decided to taint their ranks." My lip curled at the expression. According to the Reds, Berserker wolves such as Samuel and I, and our whole pack, were abominations, born of evil. They'd sooner allow a human in their pack than a magic born werewolf.

I knew this because my father had been one of them, until they cast him out because his true mate, a witch, bore him a child. Me.

One thing the Red pack and I agreed on: Berserker wolves were dangerous. The magic that flowed in our blood inspired killing rage.

Like the rage I felt now. "On the mountain?"

"No. I scented him when I was on patrol, at the stream. Fergus tracked him to the edge of our land."

That settled me a little, but my lips curled away from my teeth, and I felt energy charge through me, priming me to run, to hunt, to attack.

To kill.

In the past, if a werewolf trespassed, I'd have the pack run him down and teach him a lesson. Things were different. I had a woman to protect. Neither part of me, man or beast, would allow a threat to her to live.

"I want him found and thrown in the pit. Alert me when it's done."

"As you wish, Beta." Wulfgar hefted his axe onto his

shoulder, and barked across the clearing at three other warriors lounging in wolf form. "Patrol. Now."

Trouble? I caught the echo of Samuel's voice coming to me through our shared bond. The magic that made us wolves linked our minds, and during times of strong emotion we could hear each other as clearly as if we were standing side by side.

No.

Silence reigned on Samuel's side of the bond, but he did not assert his Alpha power, which could force any wolf to bow to his will.

A possible trespasser. I sent wolves to deal with him. I pushed the words towards Samuel's mind, sending a brief impression of my worry.

I held back any feeling of anger. As Alpha, Samuel bore the brunt of the Berserker rage. When the beast took hold, he was fearsome, the most powerful of all of us. All well and good on the battlefield, but in times of peace, when the taint of magic took hold of our minds, he was the most vulnerable to losing control.

Pacing around the campfire, I waited for my swirling emotions to calm.

Daegan of Alba, Samuel spoke my name, and sent an impression of how he saw me. Dark-haired, with sinewy muscles under the furs I wore as clothes. A capable warrior. I sensed a bit of censure, as if he understood why I stayed away and tried to protect him, but didn't like it.

Come.

I wish to wait a while. I will not be responsible for your loss of control. I protested.

You are not responsible for my weakness, any more than Brenna is responsible for my strength.

She soothes the beast.

Aye. Samuel sighed. *But perhaps it is time she meets it.*

Our conversation continued as I walked down the hall carved from stone. To show Brenna the beast could mean her death. But if we held back, and lost control, it was even more dangerous.

Ye remember when she met us as wolves. She'd been terrified. I'd never forget the look on her face. She'd rather face death than us in wolf form. How much more will she hate us when she meets the monster?

She doesn't hate us. Samuel assured me. *She accepts our wolf form. She will accept the beast.*

Ye have more faith in her than I.

Perhaps.

"I hate talking to ye when you're like this." I grouched as I entered our chambers. "You're so damn calm. Ever since ye tried to become a monk, whenever we argue you have this infuriating tone. You're so bloody reasonable."

"Living on bread and water in a monastery with nothing between my thoughts and madness taught me the value of reason, if nothing else.

"I thought ye hated being a monk."

"Not enough to take back my old name." Samuel had been Sigmund before his brief conversion to the White Christ. A good strong Norse name. "I spent most of a century as Sigmund, and most of this one as Samuel."

"Which do ye like better?" I was curious. We weren't talking about the pressing matter of Brenna and our future true mate, but it was a relief to converse about mundane things.

"It doesn't matter. I'm Samuel now. The old Viking is gone."

He was right. Other than his immense battle prowess, Samuel's calm and control made him fit to lead. Wulfgar had some of the same qualities-the power of the raging beast, and a steadiness and strength to back it. Too bad Siebold hadn't learned the same.

"I wish The Viking—" I referred to Siebold by his nickname, "was gone. If we offered him to Yseult--"

"No." Samuel wouldn't even joke about such a thing.

I went to the dais, and nudged a few of the pelts aside and realized Brenna wasn't sleeping.

"Where is she?"

"In the bathing chamber, washing her garments."

"Alone?"

"A few minutes won't hurt. I'll set Fergus to guard if you wish. It'll be good practice for him." Samuel watched me pace nervously. "We can't keep her cooped up forever. Much as I'd like to."

"It's dangerous."

"She must meet the pack, and learn our ways."

"Exposing her to the pack will help nothing. She's not our true mate." I snarled. "Even if we want her to be. You heard the witch?"

"I heard." Samuel sat on the dais, arms resting on his knees. Tall and broad, he looked like a giant compared to most men. The only thing that could defeat him was the rage within.

I felt a stab of anger. The witch's words made me feel helpless. The beast hated the feeling.

"Why would the runes lie?" I kicked at the woodpile we kept to light the braziers, wishing it was an enemy. For a moment the bloodlust roared in my ears. "We need her. We can't let her go, ye know that."

"I know."

I tore my hand through my hair, feeling my nails sharpen to claws. They bit into my skull, and I stopped moving, took a deep breath. Extreme emotion brought on the beast. This close to Samuel, I had to keep control.

"Forgive me, Alpha." I offered apology to offset his humiliation. Samuel was the strongest of us, being unable to control the beast rankled. "It's just...we kept her in the cave, coddled and cared for. She lacks nothing...beyond contact with the outside world." The wolf in me whined, happy in the understanding that we kept our mate safe and cared for.

Not our mate, I reminded it.

"Did Yseult tell you how many years will it be until we lose control?"

"Ye know she did not. Damn..." I tried to think of an insult more than 'witch', and couldn't. "...witch."

"Perhaps the runes did not reveal that."

"Does it matter? The beast takes over quickly, ye know that as well as I. When it does, we must be ready to send Brenna away." Or she would die. The beast did not recognize past lovers as friends. It did not recognize anything. It knew one thing: destruction. It was the destroyer. The world was mere fodder for its violent hunger.

"Is it possible—"

"No." He cut me off but I finished anyway, "she is our true mate?"

"Humans cannot mate with werewolves."

"Then what exactly have we been doing with her all this time?" I eyed the dais where we'd spent long hours ravaging our beloved. We were as gentle as we could be with her, but in the heat of passion it was easy to slip.

One day that slip might end her life.

Shuddering at my dark thoughts, I focused on Samuel's lecture.

"A true mate means three things: they can bond with us. Survive a mating bite. And can conceive."

"And give birth." I leapt on the word.

Samuel glared at me. "None of these things can happen. We won't allow them to happen."

Grasping for an argument, I started, "My mother—"

"Was a witch with great magic."

"Like Yseult. My mother was powerful in her own way. In the end, though, it wasnae enough to save her." My thoughts were so dark, I was tempted to turn into a wolf and run away. An afternoon chasing rabbits put things in perspective. Especially when followed by an evening with Brenna.

"The runes only confirm something I suspected. Brenna is not our true mate. She cannot bond with us. She cannot survive a mating bite."

"Then why did the runes tell us to find her?"

Samuel sighed, a sound full of a hundred years of hopelessness. "I do not know."

I started pacing again. "If we try to send her away, she may not go. She's too honorable."

"Then we must leave her before we lose control." Samuel's face turned to stone, and I knew he was silencing his wolf. My own wanted to howl at the thought of losing our beloved.

"The longer we wait, the more likely the beast will win." It would only take one slip, one dark night where the beast ruled, and the unthinkable would happen. The beast was merciless. It could rip through battle-seasoned warriors like a gael through a forest. What would the gael do to a flower?

Samuel took a deep breath. "We must hang on as long as we can."

"Ye cannae take it all onto yerself."

"Daegan—"

"No, Samuel."

"I am Alpha," he growled and my eyes snapped to the

floor in automatic response to his stern tone. He didn't need to show his strength for me, or anyone else, to feel it. "The pack is not stable."

"Ye take too much on yerself." I didn't meet the Alpha's eye, but my tone chastised. Of all the pack, I was the only one who could stand up to the powerful blond warrior. The pack needed me, too. If the Alpha succumbed to the Berserker rage, what chance did the rest of us have? We would follow Samuel's lead or be torn apart.

"If ye take on too much of the taint, it will weaken ye."

"It's been so long. I know what it's like," he said hoarsely.

I nodded.

"They deserve relief."

"They will get it. Our true mate will balance us, and the peace will spill into the pack. We will find her. We have to."

Even as he said it, my wolf growled in despair. Brenna is our true mate, it insisted.

No. It cannot be.

"In the meantime, we will allow Brenna to leave the cave with us. We can't keep her hidden away forever."

"No," I snapped without thinking. "It's too dangerous."

Samuel raised an eyebrow. I lowered my gaze carefully. "Alpha. I merely point out the danger of introducing our beloved to the pack."

"They will benefit from seeing her. Even if we cannot claim her as mate, her presence will give them hope."

I couldn't say anything, so I called the magic to me, and shifted. The world dissolved and came into focus again, in sharp, colorful scents. The strongest of which— a blue fog edged with red and black—came from Samuel. Melancholy, tinged with despair.

"I do not like it anymore than you do," Samuel said. "We will be at her side the whole time."

As a wolf, I fixed my Alpha with a hurt stare, making clear without words that I wished we could keep our beloved safe in the cave with us forever.

Samuel nodded sadly. "As do I."

A brief stint chasing rabbits did me good. I washed up in a mountain stream and shifted. By the time I returned to our quarters, Brenna had finished her washing. Her dress and a few furs lay on the rocks to dry, and she had entered the pool naked.

I stood in the cave of hot springs, watching her bathe. The waters filling the cavern were the reason we'd chosen to make this mountain our home. That and the rooms and tunnels crafted by dwarves long ago.

The water lapped at her reddened buttocks as she bathed. I admired the grace in her simple movements. From the first day we bought her, she had the poise and elegance of a queen.

When I had enough of watching I started into the water. She startled and whirled as if she had forgotten me. I grinned and waved a hand to see if she'd forgiven me for tanning her arse.

Her lips curved in scorn. She turned and set her back to me.

Chuckling, I settled on a rock to enjoy the view. She couldn't stay in the water forever.

When she finished bathing, I called, "Come on out, lass. I have a gift for ye."

She approached warily, and I was struck by the contrast between her pale skin, and her dark hair and fetching doe eyes. I couldn't resist pulling her into my arms and pressing a kiss to her cold lips, and stroking her hair back from the white weal on her neck. Even her scar was lovely to me, because it was a part of her.

I showed her my peace offering: a cloth filled with berries I'd picked. They won me a smile, but she folded the cloth and set it aside on the rock. My lady took my hand and pulled me to standing. She reached up and traced my features, my nose, cheeks and brow. I knew what she saw, a man of indeterminate age, dark-haired with light eyes that turned gold when the magic was upon me. Years of hard living had turned my face rawboned and rugged, but the magic that allowed us to heal quickly also extended our lives. For all its faults, the beast kept us young.

"Samuel wants ye to meet the pack." I told her. "We plan to take ye out tomorrow."

I let her stroke the worry lines on my forehead away. The wolf sighed in contentment.

"I dinnae want to expose ye, Brenna. Tis not safe. We are not..." I struggled to explain. "We are not safe."

She kept touching me. Her fingers traced my brows.

I shut my eyes, realizing then how on edge I'd been for the last few hours, waiting for her to accept or banish me. Her fingers soothed across my brow and cheeks, tracing gentle lines down to my chest. Every muscle in my body relaxed.

The wolf slept.

3

The next day, I helped her dress in her one remaining gunna, along with thick leather boots.

"Samuel has requested ye dine with the pack. You're to stay close to me or him at all times, and keep yer eyes lowered."

I checked the torc around her neck. "This marks ye as ours," I told her, "but there are limits to its protection."

Her fingers stroked the silver collar, and I felt a surge of protective pride. I kissed her, then gripped her wrist. "Come, lass."

I led her out of the cave, pausing in the entrance.

"Remember the rules, now. Dinnae look any of the pack in the eye. The wolf considers it a challenge."

Her brow wrinkled.

"I'm serious, lass. Tis a grave offense. Keep yer eyes down and keep close to me."

She frowned but stepped closer, her eyes trained on the rock at my feet.

"Good lass."

I fought my own wariness as we stepped into the clearing. Samuel had ordered all the pack to remain as men for this trial visit. Our wolf forms reminded her of her attack. So a score of men stared as they caught Brenna's scent. The other dozen would be hunting, or on patrol.

Brenna started to look up, and I softly reminded her, "Eyes."

As we moved out into the open, her heart beat faster, and her scent tinged with nervousness, which only made the men stare longer. The only thing more enticing than a beautiful, trembling woman was her fear. It screamed 'prey.'

Brenna's frightened scent tasted delicious. At this rate, I doubted we'd reach the center of the clearing before a Berserker tried to take a bite out of her.

Gripping her wrist, I drew her closer.

"Calm yerself, lass," I ordered quietly. "I willnae let harm come to ye." I glared at the others over her head. A few men ducked their head in submission.

Samuel entered the clearing, naked but for a loincloth. As his gaze swept the gathering, the rest of the warriors took care to show no interest in the Alpha's woman. They went back to tending the fire, readying a great spit for the meat, or sharpening weapons. All except Fergus who remained a wolf who tucked his head as Brenna and I passed him. If Brenna recognized the wolf with reddish brown fur as the young red head male who'd rushed at her, she made no sign.

Samuel motioned us over to where he sat on a great rock like a king on a throne. I laid a pelt at his feet and bade Brenna sit beside him. Leaning forward, he rested a hand on the back of her neck.

Once the meat was roasted, I offered Samuel the best portion. He carved with his knife and hand fed our beloved bit by bit. Her cheeks pinked enticingly, but she did not refuse any of his offerings.

Either Samuel or I touched her often, trying to keep a hand on her at all times. Claiming her. Showing the pack she could behave.

She kept her eyes lowered, even when the warriors started one of their favorite games, throwing their axes at a log Wulfgar had dragged up the mountain. Siebold made Fergus, the smallest and weakest of the pack, collect the axes. Samuel allowed this show of dominance, though he watched carefully.

In wolf form, Fergus carried the axe back and set it at Siebold's feet. He trotted back to the target when the very axe he'd returned sliced by him, nearly catching his tail.

Fergus yipped and ran.

Siebold laughed until a small metal tipped spear sliced his shoulder. Outraged he looked for the thrower. Wulfgar stood with arms folded, glowering. Siebold was fourth in pack hierarchy, and not for lack of trying to be third. Wulfgar had bested the blond warrior more than once.

Gritting his teeth, Siebold pulled the spearhead from his flesh. Blood spurted down his bare muscles. He didn't take his eyes off Wulfgar's.

Wulfgar growled in challenge.

Beside me Brenna gasped.

The spell was broken; Siebold glanced at our beloved, golden eyes bright.

I realized Brenna was staring at the blond warrior. I shoved her head down.

Still angry, Siebold took a step towards Brenna. Samuel was on his feet in an instant, with a roar that shook the mountain. Half the pack dropped to all fours, starting to shift. I pulled Brenna up with an arm secured around her neck. She gripped my forearm, her head turning to my chest, her eyes squeezed shut.

This was a verra bad idea.

Samuel snarled at the pack. If he lost control now—

Luck arrived in the form of a small red wolf. Fergus ran back into the gathering, barking news.

Intruder...at the foot of the mountain.

Tension, already high, rippled through the pack. As one the warriors rose, grabbing their weapons.

"Wulfgar, Siebold, with me." Samuel's eyes glittered gold. I felt his fury, the beast pounding at the wall of control Samuel kept high at all times.

Samuel, perhaps I should go instead, I spoke along the brother bond. He turned his furious expression on me and I bowed my head at his show of power.

"Get her inside," he ordered. *Before the intruder catches her scent.*

"Come, Brenna." I cursed myself as I pulled her along. Her first time with the pack, and she gave challenge to Siebold, and then attracted an intruder? The excursion couldn't have gone any worse.

At the mouth of the cave, Brenna tugged at my hand, forcing me to face her. She put a hand on my arm, face contorted with a worried expression.

"He'll be alright lass. Save yer worry for any intruder. They'll face the Alpha's wrath." She nodded and accepted my kiss, though she still looked concerned. "Do ye truly believe Samuel will be hurt?" I teased gently. "Have a little more faith in your Berserker mates." The word 'mate' rolled off my tongue before I could catch it.

We were halfway to our chambers when I heard something following us. I whirled and thrust Brenna behind me at the same time.

The little red wolf slinking after us whined in apology.

"Och, 'tis only Fergus. "

Fergus dropped a leather pouch at my feet.

"I thank ye," I told the little wolf. Fergus gave a toothy grin and loped off. I opened and grinned at the small polished wooden object inside. "Finally, something good on this shite day." Both Brenna and I needed a distraction, and now I had it. I grabbed Brenna's hand and tugged her to the bathing chamber to play with our new toy.

"TELL ME, Brenna, what do ye think of this last visit to the pack?" I asked as soon as we reached the bathing pool.

She pressed her lips together. Her first sight of the pack, she'd almost run screaming off the mountain.

"Ye did well, up until the end when ye were staring at Siebold. Tell me truly: did you look him in the eye?"

Brenna crossed her arms in front of her before she nodded.

"I thought so. As much as I'd like to give that piker a good thrashing, rules are rules. Wulfgar or another wolf might let yer behavior pass, but Siebold will demand punishment."

I ran a soothing hand down her stiff back.

"Dinnae be afraid. Ye learn our ways, soon enough." I squeezed her bottom through her dress. "I dinnae want to warm yer bottom so soon after yer last spanking. But I have a little reminder for ye to keep our commands." I stepped back. "Take off yer clothes." I smacked her bottom to urge her along, and went and got supplies to shave her smooth.

Naked, Brenna took her place in front of me on the rock, lying back with her knees bent and feet flat on the stone.

I settled in, running a finger down her pink lower lips, enjoying the sight and feel of slight fuzz. Shaving her was usually my chore and delight, and she was used to it. Both Samuel and I enjoyed the feel of her silky skin.

"Legs wide apart," I ordered, even though she'd already spread wide enough. With a sigh, she obeyed, waiting placidly for me to get on with it. She twisted her fingers together but other than that showed no sign of nervousness.

With great care I honed the blade. I took my time oiling her plump lips, running a thumb up and down until her breathing quickened. She shifted her bottom on the stone and I pinched her. "Be still, lass."

I heard her huff above my head, and lowered mine to hide a grin. Her cunny flushed and her little nub perked up, ready for my attentions once my task was done.

When her cunny was smooth, I ran my oiled hands up her legs. She'd shaved them herself, earlier, and I enjoyed the silky skin, massaging and pressing a few kisses from ankle to knee.

Brenna spread her legs even wider as if inviting me to spend more time at her center. After shaving her I usually teased her to an orgasm or two.

Brenna look disappointed when I stood up and sat beside her.

"Ye did well. Almost done. Come lie across my lap, there's a good lass."

She moved with alacrity, no doubt expecting a reward.

I checked her lower lips. I played in her folds until I felt her quicken, then my fingers strayed higher, to the cleft of her bottom. I often squeezed and parted her cheeks and teased her lower hole. She allowed it, assuming I just enjoyed her bottom.

Today I would enjoy it even more. Today the little

wooden plug lay beside her on a cloth, waiting its turn. Carved and polished to a sheen, it would look beautiful nestled between her bum cheeks. With enough oil, it would slip right into her back passage.

After a few minutes massaging her cheeks, I oiled the little wooden bulb and set the narrow end at her pucker.

Immediately she tensed.

"Shhh, easy. There's a good lass."

She squirmed and I swatted her bottom.

"Be still. Ye didna think I would let yer behavior earlier go unpunished? Whenever ye break the rules yer bottom pays the price one way or another. You'll wear the plug now, and next time we go out among the pack. And one day, you'll be stretched enough for me and Samuel to take ye together."

"Deep breath, lass. This is a reminder for ye, and a reward for Samuel."

And me, I added silently.

With a little more uncomfortable twitching, she allowed me to plug her behind. My cock hardened at the sight of the wooden end seated well inside her. "Well done, Brenna."

I checked her lower lips and held my fingers in front her face. "Just as I suspected. Ye liked that more than ye let on."

She started struggling again, and I trapped her legs under one of mine. "Now for yer reward."

My fingers rubbed her little nubbin until she squirmed and panted for a different reason. I brought her to the brink again and again, stopping before she went over. Each time I paused I twisted the plug, training her to get used to movement inside her sweet arse. From the way she gasped and jerked her hips, she didn't altogether dislike it.

Finally I stroked her little nub. "Come, Brenna."

When she'd shuddered to completion, I helped her up.

"Ye did well." I said. "Ye please me."

I turned her and checked the plug. The sight of the wood winking from between her cheeks made me hard. Seated deep inside her, it would stretch her bottom hole.

"You will wear this as a reminder that ye belong to us." I gripped her bottom hard and smacked it before leaving her to clean up the shaving supplies.

"Soon Samuel will return. Until then perhaps we can find a way to spend the afternoon."

I turned around just in time to see the plug sail into the water and disappear with a splash.

"Brenna." I kept my tone stern, but just barely.

She faced me, chin high and arms crossed over her chest. Even naked and flushed from all our play, she looked proud as a queen.

I walked by her, smacking her bottom as I passed. She jumped but didn't change her stance. "Naughty, naughty, lass. Now ye will be punished. Samuel will be back soon, and he'll find ye with a bright red arse."

A few minutes searching about the pool for the plug, and I gave up in disgust. Brenna backed away when I stalked from the water, but her few steps of retreat were no match for my burst of speed, and she was over my shoulder in a second. "Fergus carved that plug for ye. Do ye think he cannae make another?"

I carried her to our sleeping chamber and laid her on the dais. "Stay."

In a moment I was back at her side, a long strip of cloth in my hand. I bound her hands and stretched them over her head, securing her at the base of the dais. We'd installed an iron ring in anticipation of an unruly prize. So far Brenna had proved to be compliant; there'd been no reason to shackle her.

Until now.

Tousling my wet hair to dry it faster, I grinned down at her. "Normally I'd wait for Samuel to return and decide a fitting punishment, but he's indisposed. We'll just have to entertain ourselves until he gets back."

She watched me warily as I positioned myself at her feet.

"Open yer legs, lass, or I'll tie them apart."

Her breathing quickened as she exposed herself to my gaze. The subtle scent of her desire wafted towards me and I gave an exaggerated sniff, waggling my eyebrows at her when she blushed. Being tied up seemed to excite her.

I wasted no time planting my mouth right on her center, warming every sweet inch with my hot breath. She arched her body, pushing her hips up so her cunny pressed against my mouth. She hadn't been expecting this, and wanted to take advantage of it.

Swiveling my head, I let my tongue glide in a circle around her swollen nub. North, East, South, West, my tongue went anywhere but the one place she longed for me to taste.

Her hips jerked, begging for more. Her juices ran down into the crevice of her cheeks. I scooped some of the silky secretion and coated one finger before I probed gently at her bottom hole. Suddenly she was squirming backwards.

Grasping her ankles, I pulled her back down.

"No, no, lass. There's more than one way to train ye to take us back here. And you're going to like it."

I spanked her cunny just hard enough to make her gasp. Her eyelids fluttered in shocked pleasured. I did it again, alternating slaps with teasing rubs.

Holding her legs open, I continued worshiping at the shrine of her slick, wet cunt, enjoying the way her lips plumped under my tongue's ministrations. I delved deeper, fluttering inside her sopping hole before tracing a trail down between her buttocks. This time, my tongue probed her lower hole.

She gave token resistance, but her struggles died down as my fingers stroked her labia. She wriggled anew when I thumbed her swollen clit. My tongue forced its way past the tight ring of muscle; I fucked her arse with my tongue and pleasured her with my hand. Her legs lay over my shoulders as I burrowed deeper into her tiny hole. Her upper body twisted, but the bonds on her wrists held fast. I was merciless. Her feet slapped my back as she writhed.

Brenna came hard, her entire body trembling.

"A few more of those, and you'll be cumming from a finger in your arse alone." I slipped my little finger into her bum and twisted it. She shuddered, but her face was lax with pleasure.

"We'll claim every part of ye. Soon," I said, and lowered my head for another round.

4

H ours later Samuel reached out through the bond. *Daegan?*

I'm here. I rose from the dais. *Good hunt?*

Aye. We found the intruder. He's in the pit.

I smiled at the mental image of the clearing at the base of the mountain, with the mouth of a deep hole gaping at its center. Wolves stood guard around the premises.

We'll leave him in there a few days before questioning him.

I focused on Brenna, who had roused from her nap. I'd spent the afternoon pleasuring her before giving her a sound spanking for tossing the plug. I'd taken her until she'd climaxed around my cock, and we'd cuddled and slept.

Now she watched me, keen to my sudden stillness. Not much escaped her. Even though she had no voice to ask a question, I had a feeling she knew all our secrets.

"Samuel's returned. He's looking forward to seeing ye."

She reached for her dress and I snatched it up and withheld it. "Do ye think you've earned clothes today? Naughty lassies stand in the corner, their red arse on display."

With a sigh, she withdrew her hand.

I reached out to Samuel along our mental path, and gained reassurance that he was close to returning.

Instead of the corner, I positioned Brenna on the dais, on her knees with her head lowered and buried in her arms. Her bottom pointed for the door, a treat for Samuel.

When the Alpha arrived, he paused in the entryway, golden eyes brutal and brutish. I held my breath. So did Brenna.

Who was dominant-the warrior or the wolf?

Samuel stalked forward and circled the dais, like a predator on the hunt. Brenna remained frozen in position. The Alpha ran a finger down Brenna's back. His touch was light but she shivered. Her skin prickled all over, with magic or anticipation, or both.

"Spread your legs." Samuel's voice rasped like he'd forgotten its use.

Brenna obeyed, her head still planted in the furs.

Samuel examined her, grasping her buttocks, pulling them apart. Our beloved's hands fisted in the pelts but she didn't move.

"You used the plug."

"Aye."

Samuel glanced at me, his hands still prising Brenna's arse cheeks apart. "How did it go?"

"I turned my back and Brenna...lost it."

Still kneeling behind her, Samuel gathered a skein of our beloved's hair, wrapping it around his wrist until her back arched and head drew back. Over and over, he murmured her name. "Brenna, Brenna, Brenna. How will I fuck your arse if it is not stretched to take me?"

Her body bowed backwards to ease the strain on her hair. I watched her pulse flutter in her throat.

Abruptly Samuel released her, and her head fell back to the furs. Grasping her hips, he pulled her bottom flush against him, and used his cock to stroke her folds. Her breathing changed, growing ragged.

"Next time," Samuel growled, "I will not wait. You best allow Daegan to prepare you. Because I intend to take what belongs to me. And this—" His hand gripped her bottom, hard, "is mine."

With a sudden move, Samuel covered her with his body, forcing her completely down onto the furs. He kept a hand on the back of her neck and used the other to guide himself inside her. Brenna lay on her stomach, pinned and helpless. With her legs together her channel would feel tighter. My balls drew up to my body in anticipation of such a sweet fuck.

I stroked myself watching Brenna's body shudder with the Alpha's fierce thrusts into her welcoming body. I knew the moment she climaxed, thrashing against the furs. Her fists opened and closed. Samuel sped up, his hips beating against hers.

I focused on Brenna's face even as visions flashed through my mind. The speed of the wolf on the hunt. Brenna, the skin of her back whipped red. The desire to do violence flooded through me, stealing my breath.

Samuel cried out.

Unable to hold back, I spent myself on the stone. I tore myself from the wall, wondering at what I'd seen. On the dais, Samuel sagged over our beloved, clutching her to him.

Wrenching myself away, I left the cave and headed down the mountain.

～

HALFWAY DOWN, I realized my hands were shaking. I paused and the wolf was quiet. The beast was curious, watchful, waiting. What had I seen?

My mother had been a witch to rival Yseult's power, but instead of seeking to enslave a werewolf, my mother fell in love with one. My father lay with her, and she bore him a son. Me. But my father's pack never trusted my witch mother. Afraid she might use the pack bonds for her purposes, my father's pack tore out her throat. My father secreted me away, only later introducing me to his pack. But it was too late. I was not just a werewolf. I was a Berserker—witchborn, tainted by magic. The power coursing through me was a blend of my mother and father's. Together it created a monster.

For all my power—the ability to shift, to rage, to link with my Alpha and pack—I'd never had a vision before. Some of it was in the past, I was sure. Some of it the future. Each image seemed a sign of what was to come, but when they all came to pass, what would happen?

Cursing the gods, I loped down the mountain path. Unexplained, the vision would only torment me. Luckily, I had a prisoner to take it out on.

WULFGAR MET me at the base of the mountain. The warrior sniffed the air, and a grin cracked his brutish features.

I smelled of sex.

Cursing, I detoured to a mountain stream to wash my beloved's scent away. Wulfgar followed, chuckling. "How did it go? Did she struggle as she took the plug?"

I wanted to snarl that it was none of his concern but I caught the longing in his eye. Wulfgar had been alone as long as Samuel. And he was a faithful warrior. He deserved some details, though not enough to torture him.

"She didn't like it."

"No?"

"She threw it in the pool."

Wulfgar's guffaw echoed off the mountain.

"Fergus and I had a bet as to what would happen." The warrior shook his shaved head. "That little red wolf was right."

It was inevitable that the pack discussed our beloved, but I didn't like it. After dipping my head in the freezing waterfall, I left the pool. "How is the prisoner?"

"Still trapped in the pit. I have a guard on him."

"I wanted to check on him, make sure he doesn't die before we get answers."

Wulfgar nodded in understanding. The pack usually saved their brutality for the battlefield, but it had been a long time since they'd had a war to entertain them.

I picked up the pace, jogging towards the clearing where we'd dug the pit. Wulfgar followed.

"The guards have instructions not to engage with the prisoner."

"Who is he?"

"No idea. But he's a fine black wolf. Led us a merry chase before we cornered him and drove him here."

We broke into the clearing where warriors ranged around the pit. A fire burned a few feet away, the scent of roasting meat its own form of torture for a trapped and starving man.

And all but one guard stepped aside. Siebold had his back to us as he urinated into the gaping black hole in the earth.

"Siebold," Wulfgar barked. "You're off duty."

The blond shot him a look of fury and spat into the pit before he slunk away.

I took Siebold's place, peering into the deep black hole. We'd spent three days digging, and shoring up the steep sides to create a prison that would hold a Berserker. If man or beast tried to climb out, the pit might collapse and bury him in an early grave.

"Light." I held up my hand in order, and Wulfgar handed me a torch lit from the nearby fire. "Who threw spears down there?"

When no one spoke I knew the answer.

"Siebold must have when I left. Rabbit-brained bully," Wulfgar sniffed the insult with absolute disdain. "I'll order him and the others to stay back from the pit, no matter what."

"Ye think he can throw the spears this far?" I handed the torch back. The prisoner had stepped out of the shadows into the circle of sunlight.

"Better not to take a chance. I don't know what the warrior is capable of. He's in wolf form."

As I watched the black wolf shifted into a man. "Not anymore."

The warrior had black hair, and powerful shoulders inked blue. I'd seen a few warriors bear such marks. He tossed his head as he shook off the magic of the change. "Is this the sort of welcome I receive from the Berserker pack?"

"We dinnae take kindly to strangers on our mountain," I called down.

The warrior smirked. He stood proud and cocky for a prisoner in a pit. "Your mountain? I thought all Berserkers were changed by a witch in the North Lands. You sound like a native of Alba."

"I was born here, aye." I didn't mind giving details to a dead man. "Who are you?"

"They call me Maddox. I hail from a clan not far from here."

"The Red pack?"

"No." He grinned. "We are Berserkers, also."

Chills ran up my spine. Besides our pack, there were no other Berserker wolves. I took a moment to convey Maddox's claim to Samuel. Maddox watched with a half smile, as if he knew why I paused.

He claims he's a Berserker.

Impossible. Unless--

"Who is yer Alpha?" I asked the prisoner.

"Ragnvald."

A Norse name. No wonder this Maddox knew our history. Rangvald was most likely a Viking Berserker, like Samuel, Siebold and Wulfgar, and most of the pack— besides Fergus and I.

"Ask Sigmund if he'll speak with me now."

"There is no Sigmund here," I tested the wolf.

Maddox let out a barking laugh. "Sigmund was Samuel's name before he took vows to follow the white Christ. The name stuck, even if his faith didn't."

He knows. I relayed back to Samuel, feeling a prickle of trepidation.

Maddox smiled, showing all his teeth. "Ragnvald told me."

"How does Ragnvald know Samuel?"

"Because Ragnvald is Bodolf's son. And Bodolf was Samuel's Alpha, once."

5

"There's another pack of Berserkers." I stormed into our chambers, where Samuel sat on the dais, elbows to knees and a thoughtful look on his face. "How can this be?"

The Alpha put a finger to his lips and glanced down at Brenna. Our woman slept, wrung out from our exertions and her many orgasms, no doubt.

"The witch turned several dozen of us," Samuel said. "Bodolf led us until we sailed East to this island. I led a contingent, Bodolf and his son, another. I did not know what happened to them. I thought they'd been slain."

"Obviously only Bodolf was. His son lives, and wishes to take residence near us. Who knows how many warriors he leads."

"This Maddox...he is like you, Daegan? Mothered by a witch? Is that how he came to bear the Berserker taint?"

"I don't know." I pictured the tattooed prisoner, smirking up at me from the pit. Like Siebold, I wanted to piss on his face. "He is not of Alba."

Samuel stroked his chin. "The tattoos you describe remind me of the warriors that hail from an island further east."

"All I know is that he is a Berserker. And he wants to speak to you."

Voices in the corridor interrupted us.

"Yes?" Samuel called.

Fergus shuffled in, his eyes on the ground. His punishment over, he'd been allowed to return to man form, but he kept careful deference to the Alpha. He shifted from foot to foot.

"Report," I ordered.

"We've been summoned. To the Thing. A runner met me on the far reach of my patrol."

Another visitor in so short a time. I didn't like it.

"Who?" Samuel asked.

"One of the Red Pack. He would not tell me his name, nor get close." Fergus flashed a smile, even though he did not lift his eyes from the stone. The runt of our pack, he was still stronger and faster than most other werewolves. He'd been bullied so long it would please him to be able to intimidate another.

"When does the Red Pack wish to meet?"

"Not this full moon, but the next," Fergus said, and Samuel dismissed him.

"No doubt the Red Pack wishes us to deal with the new Berserkers."

"Of course, if we fight them, we may be so evenly matched that we both lose a great number of wolves."

"The Red Pack can only hope."

"So ye will go?"

"No. You will."

I tensed. "Is that wise?"

"I can trust you to hold your temper." He rose. "Come. I've called a warrior to guard our beloved. We will speak with this Maddox together."

WULFGAR AND FERGUS stood guard at the foot of the mountain.

"I take it the pack knows of our invitation to the Thing?"

Fergus had the grace to look sheepish.

I clapped the smaller warrior on the shoulder. "Dinnae be dismayed. We will need yer wagging tongue to accompany me to the Thing."

"Are you sure?" Wulfgar asked, and the stare he fixed on me made it clear he wasn't asking if it was wise for Fergus to go, but me.

"My Alpha commands. The Red Pack will never take me unawares again."

Wulfgar's forehead creased. "I'm not concerned about whether you should watch your back. I wonder if they should watch theirs."

"We'll find out then." I gave him a toothy grin. I had a score to settle with the Red Pack. Wulfgar and everybody knew it. But the Reds wanted our attendance, and Samuel no longer trusted himself to be level-headed around so many potential enemies, so I would go. We could only hope my own control didn't break. The beast so loved revenge.

We reached the pit. With a gesture, Samuel bade us all stay back. He alone went to peer down at the man.

I moved as close as I could without breaking my Alpha's command. If the encounter upset him and Samuel's beast broke free, I would be close enough to do something. Even die.

"Maddox. I am Samuel, once named Sigmund. Speak."

"Alpha." The prisoner's tone, at least, was respectful. "Bodolf's son Ragnvald sends his greetings."

"It's been a long time since I heard that name. I wonder now why I am hearing it again."

"Ragnvald has looked for you these past few decades. He knows you left his father Bodolf's pack, and severed the Alpha bond. He wishes to make peace."

"By sending you to trespass on our land?"

"I am a Berserker. I fear no one."

"Perhaps you should, Maddox of Ragnvald's clan. Tell me, where are you from?"

"Ériu," Maddox named an island to the east of us. "I was cursed by a witch to bear the Berserker rage. I came to fight for a king, and Ragnvald found me. He taught me to train my beast."

"And what of Ragnvald now? Does he control his beast, or does the beast control him?"

Maddox's silence told us the answer.

"How long ago did Ragnvald lose control?" Samuel's voice was deceptively gentle.

"Three moons. Ragnvald has since gained the upper hand but—"

"But will lose it again. It's only a matter of time. His father succumbed to the rage."

"Ragnvald killed him."

"I wondered what had happened to Bodolf. So now—" Samuel's tone hardened. "You come to me, to beg me to save Ragnvald? Knowing how dangerous it is for one Alpha to best another? Did you really think I'd risk my life, and the sanity of my pack for a warrior I abandoned long ago?"

"I had hoped you would remember him as a brother."

"No," Samuel said, and reached out, beckoning to me. I went and stood next to my Alpha, frowning down at the prisoner. "Daegan is my brother. Ragnvald and I were rivals, at best. I'm surprised he didn't tell you."

"He did." Maddox stood straight-backed, inked shoulders set as if he were entering a fight instead of looking up at his captors from the bottom of a pit. "I had hoped the centuries would've mellowed you."

"I am a Berserker. We do not grow weak."

"The beast makes the strongest of us weak. I have seen it. A great warrior, leader, friend...now slavering like a dog. I keep him chained in a cave, away from the pack. If one of them were to stray, or if he were to break loose and come for us, a link to his mind would be enough to pull us all into madness." Naked pain crawled over Maddox's face.

I did not have to hear Samuel's thoughts to know what my Alpha wanted to do. Saving Ragnvald would satisfy him, if only because the warrior would be indebted to him. Beyond that, it pleased Samuel to preserve a link to his past. And there was the part of him that wanted to save a man's life for the sake of saving it.

I felt Samuel harden himself to Maddox's pleas. In this moment, my Alpha would prove why he was a true leader.

"I am sorry," Samuel said. "You have done a great thing for your warrior brother."

"But you will not help."

"I cannot. If you live long enough to survive Ragnvald, and become Alpha, you'll understand. I will not risk many for one." Both Samuel and I turned away from the pit.

Maddox called after us, his voice cracking. "We have a wolf in our pack who reads runes. He told us there is a woman for us."

I stopped in my tracks, and Samuel gripped my shoulder to keep me from flying back, demanding Maddox say more.

Could Brenna be the mate for these other wolves?

No. It cannot be. We willnae allow it.

"I know you have a secret." Maddox said. "I scent her on you."

Annoyance turned to fear within me.

Control yourself, Samuel ordered me. *He does not know who she is to us.*

With a hand signal, Samuel ordered us all away from the pit. Maddox kept shouting.

"I know she isn't just a whore you picked up from the village. Ragnvald has dreamt of her—our volva. You must let me speak to her!"

Samuel turned before I could stop him, and raced back to teeter on the edge of the pit. "The only thing I must do is decide whether or not to cover this pit with a stone. The rain will be a mercy, until hunger eats you alive. Be silent, or I will order the pack to cover this pit with a rock, and you will never see the sun again."

I felt the Alpha's rage building, the taint spreading, silencing his wolf, swallowing his humanity until the only thing left was the beast—

Samuel. I choked out. *Give yer rage to me.*

The Alpha roared.

I shifted, and ran and ran and ran. Samuel's blast of power overtook me and I felt my wolf self change—nails lengthening, body reshaping—so I was neither man nor wolf but something else.

"What is the beast?" Yseult once asked us. "Man or wolf?"

"Neither." I'd answered, at the same time Samuel said, "Both. The focus of the wolf and cruelty of the man."

"What comes of such a union?"

"Ragnarok." Samuel had answered. "The end of worlds."

The end of my world, I thought, before the beast claimed my mind.

6

I woke in the center of a circle of destruction. Saplings and bushes ripped from the ground. The earth torn where great claws had ripped into it. My hands bore cuts lined with dried blood. The magic healed quickly, but I still ached.

Beside me lay the carcass of a stag, a powerful creature with a giant rack of antlers. A hundred spears would have to work to bring it down. The head lay several feet away from its body. Its entrails spilled in a gruesome feast for ravens.

I stood, stretching painful muscles. The elk wasn't the only casualty. Carcasses of animals littered the ground. Rodents, sparrows, even beetles, nothing survived the maelstrom of Berserker rage. The earth stank of tainted magic.

At least I was alive. Samuel once told me about a Berserker who, after a great battle, clawed his own heart out. Others cut their flesh with knives. What else had I done?

There was no sight of the mountain. I had run for miles. Luckily I could easily follow the beast's path.

I headed home, but my steps faltered. When the beast was upon us, it took our sight, our vision, our sanity. Our woman would never survive. Our only hope was to stay away. It would be better if I never returned.

Do not think such thoughts, Samuel ordered. *Come home. She misses you.*

I obeyed. I did not know how Samuel could be so calm. To him, Brenna was the last hope of a dying man.

And his control had to be perfect.

By dusk I limped up the mountain. Samuel met me at the mouth of the cave.

"How long was I gone?"

"Three days. I am sorry," he said, before loping away. He would spend a day off the mountain, part in penance, in part to distance himself from the rage simmering underneath all my control.

I found Brenna in a chamber we'd given her for her own. Long ago, whoever had carved the rooms out of stone had cunningly found ways to let air and light flow in from the outside. Brenna's little room had a patch of sunlight from late morning until afternoon. The place stayed warmer than any other, besides the cavern of hot springs.

My footsteps were silent on the stone floor. Our beloved knelt over a patch of earth we'd gathered for her, tending to her garden. I'd never believed flowers would grow inside a cave, but Brenna probably could coax them from the very stone.

"Hello, lass."

She started at my voice, and again when she saw me. I must've looked rougher than I felt, for she came to my side and threw my arm around her shoulders to guide me to the bathing chamber. There, she washed her hands before gripping mine and leading me into the pool.

I didn't realize how my head was pounding until her fingers stroked my hair. I stood with my eyes closed as she soaped a cloth and rubbed my·tired muscles. When she bade me dunk, I obeyed and came out of the water feeling like a new man.

"Brenna." I wanted to touch her, but I felt I did not deserve her. I held out my hands to her, wondering how I could explain, wondering how much Samuel had told her.

She took a step towards me, then another. I realized it didn't matter. Even if we tried to keep a secret from her, somehow she knew. Her hands gripped mine.

My control snapped. I pulled her into my arms, and she let me, her body soft and pliant. Her fingers danced over my jaw, reminding me to be gentle. My own fingers fisted in her hair, drawing her head back for a kiss. I claimed her mouth until her cheeks were scraped raw from my stubble.

Lifting her, I strode quickly to our chambers. When the Berserker rage took me, I'd lain on the cold forest floor. I wanted her in the softness of the furs. The simple pleasures reminded me of my humanity.

In her arms I would remember who I was. I would remember who I still could be.

Inside our chambers, I set Brenna down and backed her to the dais. She lay willingly, and opened her legs.

Brenna's gown was wet, so I stripped it off her. The fabric tore in my haste. "Sorry, lass. I'll buy ye another. I'll buy ye a hundred more, so ye have plenty left when I rip them off."

I bent my head to her breast. Our beloved's body arched and undulated beneath my questing mouth. Her breathing grew harsh as I worked lower, finding her most secret places and exploring them with my tongue. Her soft gasps filled the chamber.

"I missed ye, Brenna." A kiss to her ankle, and I nibbled my way back up to her center. Brenna lay limp, already sated by one orgasm. "I need ye. I want yer scent all over my body." I rubbed my face in her secret folds, holding her down by her hips as she fought to get away. "One whiff of me and the pack will know I am yers." Brenna's body shook under me as pleasure rolled through her. She still writhed as I flipped her over and pushed my cock into her. "I cannae get enough of this. Never, never." I groaned as I rocked in and out of her. She was wet and ready, her liquid heat flowing in rivers over my cock. I pulled out and paused before slamming into her. Her body slid forward over the furs. I did it thrice more before she fought her way to hands and knees. Fisting her hands in the pelts, she pushed back against me. We worked in rhythm. Our hips slapped together and I felt my balls tighten at the sound.

"You're gonna take all I give ye." Pushing my body forward, I forced her flat onto the furs. She stilled when my mouth found the tender place between her neck and shoulder.

Mark her. My wolf growled. *Claim her. Our mate.* My head burst with the pain of fighting the desire to bite down.

Brenna huddled underneath me, her head bent forward in surrender. My mouth watered at the sight of her, the fall of her dark hair, the creamy slope of her shoulder.

"Nay," I barked, and wrenched myself up. Brenna looked back in concern.

I felt Samuel's presence at my back.

"Do you have it under control?"

Cursing, I rose. My cock was painfully hard. I would rather rip open my own chest than deny myself like this.

"Go," Samuel said. "Get the beast under control."

"Tis not the beast," I gasped. "The wolf wants to mark her." I realized we were speaking out loud and covered my mouth with my hand.

What was happening? Her presence both restored and

took all our control. Would it ever be safe to lie with her again?

Brenna sat watching us, naked but for the fall of her long, dark hair. She rose and padded towards us.

"Nay." I held out my hand to stop her. Ignoring it, she pressed herself against my body. This time, her mouth touched mine, then worked down my neck and chest. I clenched my fists as arousal spread through me. Her teeth grazed my collarbone. I sucked in a breath. More than anything I wanted her to bite down, to claim me. A mating bite from a human. What did it mean?

She kissed down my body, going to her knees. When she nuzzled the crevice between my cock and legs, my fingers clenched in her thick hair.

Samuel started forward, and I growled without taking my eyes off Brenna. She knelt before me, her head tipped back and throat exposed, nothing but desire in her eyes.

My fingers loosened in her hair, just enough for her to lean forward and capture my cock in her mouth. I kept a hand at her head, but she moved freely, licking up and down my shaft before swallowing it down.

My knees almost gave out. I tugged Brenna's head back and used her hair to draw her to her feet. Samuel stepped close to her, steadying our beloved as I lifted her into my arms and set her on my cock. Her arms tangled around my shoulders as I moved her hips up and down, forcing my shaft deep inside her. Samuel pressed closer. His eyes met mine.

Ye can take her ass.

Samuel nodded.

Now, brother.

I knew the second his finger slid into our beloved's tight back channel. Between my cock and the intrusion in her virgin hole, she bucked wildly. Her nails clawed my back as her orgasm claimed her.

I came with a roar. I ended up on my knees, Brenna's body still shuddering as I cradled her.

Samuel stood by, wiping his hand on a rag while wearing a smug smile.

~

THE NEXT FEW days and nights, I fucked and slept, woke in Brenna's arms and did it all over again. Samuel brought us food and watched over us, but did not take his own pleasure. There was no danger of him losing control in the throes of passion, but it was his form of penance.

As for me, I found my absolution in Brenna's arms. When I left the cave one night, I felt peace where the rage had been.

The moon shone high in the sky as I left our chambers and our beloved asleep on the furs.

I found Samuel near the prisoner's pit. On his orders, the pack had doused the bonfire. The Alpha squatted near the charred remains. He rose when he saw me, and indicated that we should keep far away from the pit. If Maddox heard us, he did not cry out or plead for mercy. I wondered if anyone had bothered to feed him.

In silence, Samuel and I climbed the mountain until we looked out on the valley washed in silvery light. The Alpha dismissed the lookout, and waited until the warrior had trotted out of earshot before he took his place on top of the look-out rock. I leaned against it.

Samuel broke the silence first. "Do you remember the day the witch told us there was a woman for us?"

"Aye." I let my head fall back against the stone. Samuel

had been barely human, his control worn thread thin. Unable to shift into the wolf at whim—a fact I'd hid from the rest of our pack. Another moon and I would've tricked Samuel into the pit, imprisoning the threat, much like Maddox had when he chained his Alpha up.

"Yseult was so smug. I could barely believe she told the truth."

"And then ye remembered the village you'd passed through. A dark-haired woman, tall and lovely, who wore a scarf around her neck." I stepped away from the rock to look up at Samuel. "Ye told me ye followed her that evening. She went into the forest, where she stripped and bathed in secret. And there ye saw her scars."

"She was mesmerizing. Fearless. I almost took her there."

"I remember teasing ye, asking why ye stopped."

There was enough moonlight to reveal the smile playing around Samuel's mouth. "You asked me if I'd taken a vow of celibacy."

"Ye were a monk."

"Not anymore. I don't know if I fully explained why I left her then, but knew instantly she was the woman the runes spoke of. When I first saw Brenna..."

He paused and I waited.

"I couldn't take my eyes from her," he whispered. "I didn't know who she was, or if she was meant for us, but I felt something. A connection, a reverence. I'd never worshiped truly until that moment. "

"Why are ye telling me this?" I asked, even though I could guess.

"Do you think we chose wrong? Perhaps the runes—"

"No. The gods are playing a joke on us, to give us a woman we cannae have." I climbed up beside Samuel, so the moonlit world lay at my feet as well as his. "I'm not giving her up. We will find a way to keep her. We must."

Samuel sighed, and nodded.

We stood there a long time, waiting for the first crease of red light on the edge of the world. When it came, I blinked like a man awake for the first time. "We need to get back. She shouldn't wake alone."

Samuel led the way, but before we came in view of the pack's bonfire, he stopped.

"When my beast overpowers me, take our woman to her sisters. Give the eldest all the money we have, and make them take Brenna far, far away, to a place we cannot follow.

I felt a chill. He hadn't said 'if', but 'when.' "Samuel—"

"Promise me, brother."

"Ye dinnae know—"

Promise me, Samuel roared in my mind.

I bowed my head. "I promise," I said finally. "I will help Brenna escape. But I will search for our true mate. And I will find her, and bring her back here. And she will give us peace."

Samuel nodded. "Very well." It was a nice dream to cling to, even if it probably wouldn't come to pass. "I've decided what to do with the prisoner." His expression told me he regretted what he was about to tell me.

"It's the only choice," I said. "We cannae risk him bringing tales of Brenna back to his Alpha."

"It will be slow. The rain will keep him alive for a time. But he hasn't had flesh to eat for days, besides his own."

"We can try to spear him, as Siebold did. Perhaps I will have better aim. Or we can wait until he is weak, then pull him up and kill him."

"No." Samuel said. "Leave him to die."

When the Alpha disappeared into the cave, I lingered to

give the news to the pack. I gave orders to let the prisoner succumb to hunger. Fergus piped up.

"Can I watch?"

"No. Samuel wishes to give the wolf his dignity. Set a guard around the perimeter but tell them to keep their distance." I didn't add my disapproval of this courtesy.

"How long?" Wulfgar asked.

"Til the full moon after next." The Berserker strength would keep Maddox alive longer than a man. "By the Thing gathering, he should starve."

"We can fill the hole with earth, leave it as his grave," Fergus said. "Isn't it lucky we had the pit deep enough to hold a Berserker?"

"Not luck." Wulfgar snorted. "We dug that hole as soon as we laid claim to the mountain."

"For intruders?" Fergus asked.

"No," I spoke up. "We built it to hold Samuel."

7

Time seemed to speed up closer to the full moon. As promised, I went on a raid with a few warriors and returned with three trunkfuls of fine things for Brenna. In addition to her silver torc, I put a ruby pendant around her neck, and silver rings around her wrists. She could barely move without the metal clinking in sweet song. She preferred the gowns to the jewelry. Samuel and I liked her naked best, but for her torc.

As the moon swelled in the sky, Brenna's ardor seemed to increase to match ours. The prisoner in the pit, Samuel's fight with the beast, and even the rest of the pack faded in the face of our lust.

Even Samuel showed reluctance to leave our chambers, though he'd been adamant we must continue to bring Brenna before the pack, to train her as our consort. If she was to stay with us long term, she must grow used to being around the wolves, and them to her.

One day, I returned from the hunt and entered our chambers in wolf form. Samuel rose from the dais, where he'd been reading one of his precious books to our beloved.

I started to climb up beside them, when Brenna waved her hands, wrinkling her nose.

"You stink," Samuel explained.

Sitting back on my haunches, I gave them both a mournful look.

"She'll pout all day if I let you up here. Or worse, send us off and wear herself out washing the pelts. Never known a woman so obsessed with keeping clean."

Brenna crossed her arms over her chest and frowned at us both.

Samuel grinned, enjoying himself. Secretly we were pleased that our woman had grown used to our wolf forms. The first time she'd seen us take the wolf's shape, she'd tried to leap off the mountain.

My tongue lolling out of my mouth, I put my paw on the bed and gave my best doggy smile.

Brenna came off the dais to shoo me. Holding one hand against her nose, she pointed to the door with the other.

"That's it, little love," Samuel chuckled as he went back to his book. "Don't let him back until you've given him a good scrubbing."

I flashed a vicious set of teeth in Samuel's direction before following Brenna out of the room.

She took me to the bathing cavern, gathering up her dress when I playfully snapped at her ankles. As always she remained poised and graceful, laying out soap and a washing cloth, along with a longer robe to dry my body. I romped in the water, pretending to ignore her. She sat near the edge of the pool, waiting for me.

When I swam close to her and barked an invitation, she shook her head. I didn't blame her. She preferred washing a man to a giant, furry animal who tried to lick her face and eat the soap.

That didn't mean I wouldn't have a little fun.

I waited until she wasn't looking at me, then bounded from the pool. Brenna put up her hands in meager defense as I shook water all over her.

She fought back a smile as she shook her finger at me in mock fury. Before I could shift into a man and carry her into the water, she shot to her feet and fled.

Always up for a good chase, I ran after her into the hall. She glanced back, pure mirth on her face, and ran right into Siebold's arms.

Immediately she jerked back but the blond warrior already had her held tight. I rushed up, snarling, and Siebold released her to face me. His weapon swung up.

"Stop, wolf, or I'll gut you."

Siebold's head snapped to the side when Brenna punched him. He stared at her in disbelief and she glared back, almost falling when I pushed her aside. My wolf snarled even as I felt my gut churn. If I were in human form, I'd warn her to look down or away. The challenge shone clearly in her eyes and Siebold, bully that he was, stepped forward to meet it.

Samuel, I called, desperate.

"Siebold," the Alpha roared, and everyone's head bowed to avoid his rage.

Siebold inched back towards the mouth of the cave.

"She met my eyes." Siebold snarled. "She needs to be punished."

I pushed Brenna towards the chamber with my wolf form. She buried her hands in my wet pelt to keep from falling. We left the Alpha to deal with the warrior.

As soon as we entered the chamber, I shifted.

"Brenna, what did ye think ye were doing? Attacking a warrior in his prime?" Fear made me angry. The sight of her striking Siebold, a warrior a half foot taller and broader than her, made me sick with worry. "Ye know the rules of the pack—ye cannae fight for dominance. Ye see a warrior, ye tuck tail and run. Stay behind me."

I advanced on her and she backed up towards the dais. "Worse, ye know that Samuel is close to breaking. Now he has to calm the worst bully of the pack. He'll demand ye be punished, Brenna. And we'll have to do it, or risk letting loose the beast."

Reaching out, I gripped her around the neck, halting her retreat. Just touching her calmed me. I thumbed her cheek gently. "I ken Siebold is a bully. But no good comes from attacking him. And I can take care of myself. You can trust me to defend you."

She nodded and I released her.

I linked to Samuel. *What's the damage?*

Stone silence from the Alpha. Whatever was going on with Siebold required his full attention.

That only put me on edge.

Brenna laid a hand over my bare chest, worry crossing her face.

"Ye broke the rules, Brenna. I fear ye must be punished."

At the quiet acceptance in her face, my anger broke and bled away. I wanted to spank and punish her but now wasn't the time. She needed to feel safe.

I pulled her into my arms.

"I'm sorry, lass. I will keep my temper. I worry over Samuel, ye ken?"

She nodded.

"Stupid bully. Siebold needs a good thrashing. I'd be glad to have ye hit him, if it didn't mean danger. It'll be all right. Samuel will deal with him, and we'll spank ye and it'll be over."

She relaxed against my chest, and I felt grateful that she wasn't afraid of our discipline. Indeed, from the scent of her heat after we turned her bottom red, she rather enjoyed it. And we always made sure it ended well for her.

I sighed. "I apologize for shouting at ye. What a day."

She squeezed me tighter and I toyed with her hair, remembering shaking water all over her. "We were having fun though, weren't we?"

She hid a grin against my chest.

I reached out to Samuel and heard nothing. Probably a bad sign.

When I looked down, Brenna was studying me.

"Are ye hungry?"

She shook her head. Stepping away from me, she pulled off her dress, then went to the dais and knelt with her bottom pointed at me.

My cock hardened. I went to her and laid a hand on her back. "Ye want this? Ye want me to spank ye?"

She shrugged then, eyes lowered, she nodded.

"You feel contrite for what ye did to poor Siebold?" I teased, and got a disgusted look. I chuckled. "I jest, but it's not funny. Siebold's a mean beast. He'll want retribution. So it's up to me to take it out on yer arse."

Lowering her front to the furs, Brenna waved her behind at me. I gave it a sharp slap.

"Do ye like yer punishment so much that ye ask for it?" My fingers sought her folds and slid against the spots that gave her the most pleasure. I waited until her body rocked, fucking my fingers before I took them away, and smacked her again. "That's it, lass, ye need a firm hand to settle ye, and then give ye pleasure." I continued, alternating spanking and touching her, enjoying the jiggle of her creamy flesh when I spanked her and the little gasps and pants as I stroked her.

"Do ye like this, Brenna?"

She buried her face in the furs. I stopped and pulled her head back by her hair. It was flushed a pretty shade of pink.

"Get up." I tugged her hair until she came to stand before me, quivering with need. I chucked her under the chin. "I don't think this is truly punishment for ye, is it?"

She shook her head, a small curve to her lips.

"You want a spanking, you need to beg me for it. Show me you want to please me, wee one."

Her hand went to my cock.

I nodded, heart leaping in glee, though I kept a somber face. "There's a good lass."

She knelt. At first she toyed with me, licking and kissing my shaft while her slender fingers cupped my sack.

After a minute, I gripped a fistful of her hair and jerked it so she met my eyes. "This is not time for ye to tease me. Ye are my woman. I will teach you to mind so ye are safe."

Wide-eyed, she didn't pull away. Instead she let me plunder her mouth, my cock sliding in and out with forceful thrusts.

My hand gripped her hair harder and she moaned, sending delicious vibrations through me.

"Brenna," I gasped. She would know I was undone. She could bring me to my knees as easily as I could order her to hers.

I pulled out of her mouth just as my cum erupted from my cock, painting her face and chest with spurts. She closed her eyes and tilted her head up, accepting my seed.

"Oh love. Ye have earned yer spanking, and yer reward."

SAMUEL FOUND US TWINED TOGETHER. I'd spanked and finger fucked her until her arse was berry red, and her cunt lips were plump and ripe for the touch. I slid my finger into her arsehole before I made her cum. Then I bound her arms behind her, lay on my back and made her bounce up and down on my cock, slapping her breasts until they were pink. Her cunny clenched with each playful slap. By the time Samuel walked in, she'd cum a dozen times, and I'd cum twice. I cradled her in my arms while she dozed, kissing her breasts to soothe them from the hurt I'd caused. Brenna slept with a smile on her face.

The scent of our lovemaking hung thick in the air. Samuel walked in and sighed.

"I see you found a way to keep busy while I was gone."

I swirled my tongue around one of Brenna's cherry tipped nipples. "Aye. Thought it best to see to her, in case Siebold demands retribution, and the pack backs him." I nodded to Brenna's red arse.

"I'm afraid it won't be that easy." Samuel seated himself on the dais, stroking one of Brenna's smooth legs as he spoke. "Siebold is furious. He wants to make a public example."

I lifted my head. "That's not for him to decide. She is ours. We discipline her where we please."

"If Brenna did what Siebold claims she did, I think it's a good idea.

I snarled. Brenna jerked awake, and I laid a hand on her cheek, pressing her to my chest until her eyes fluttered closed again.

"What happened in the hallway?" Samuel asked. "Show me."

I sent the impression of my memories through our shared link.

Samuel groaned when he realized how Brenna had challenged the bigger warrior. "I'd hoped Siebold was lying."

"What was Siebold doing in our part of the cave?"

"He came to give news of the patrol. He heard splashing
and thought I was there."

I huffed my disbelief. "He was lurking, trying to start a
fight."

"Even if he was, Brenna made it worse by her actions."

"She was defending me."

"Aye, and you can defend yourself. If she'd backed down,
you'd have gotten between her and Siebold, called for me or
shifted to order him to leave. And that would be the end of
it. Right now he's telling the whole pack how the woman
challenged him."

"He wants the pack to agree with him, and force our
hand. He wants her punished publicly, like one of the pack."
I shook my head in disgust at the bully's actions.

"And she should be. If a female wolf behaved as she did,
you'd drag her to the bonfire and spank her in front of
everyone. And then continue the lesson in private."

"Brenna isnae a wolf."

"No, but we want her to take her place in the pack. She's
either ours, or not."

I paused for a moment to listen to my wolf, but it
remained silent. Challenges and fights for rivalry were how
a wolf found its place in the pack. Formal punishment was
the way the pack protected the weak from the stronger, a
way of limiting the plays for dominance that could so easily
leave wolves crippled. A pack member who was so obviously weaker—like Brenna—could submit to public
punishment as a way to placate the need for a show of
submission.

As long as the lesson did no lasting damage to our

beloved, the wolf wouldn't protest. The pack would, though, if we didn't make an example of her for challenging Siebold. If we refused, they might demand that Siebold be the one to beat her.

My wolf growled at that. *No one touches our mate but us.*

Not our mate, I reminded the wolf. Brenna shifted in my arms and I forgot my argument. Liquid brown eyes held mine. I had a feeling she'd been faking sleep all this time, to have us speak plainly.

Tipping her back, I held her gaze. "Do ye ken what ye did to Siebold, and why ye must answer for it?"

She gulped and nodded.

"I appreciate ye trying to defend me, lass, but ye could've been killed, standing yer ground with a wolf like that. You're only dominant if you're strong enough to back it. If Siebold had gotten ye alone--"

I clasped her closer, shuddering at what the sadistic warrior would do to prove his dominance. "A public punishment may be for the best."

Samuel leaned closer and caught Brenna's chin. "You will be punished, and then it is over. The pack will see you submit to us, and to the pack structure. It will help them accept you."

Flushing, Brenna looked down.

"Ye live with us, ye lives by our rules. The sooner ye learn, the easier life will be."

8

The day of Brenna's punishment dawned with me between her legs, teasing her plump folds until their honey coated my fingers. I lapped it up, bringing her to the brink of arousal again and again, but never letting her go over. The pleasure flooding her senses would make the pain easier to bear.

Samuel entered the room. "It is time."

When we stepped out of the cave, the whole pack had assembled to watch. Almost forty wolves sat in the clearing, lounging against the rocks or crouching near the fire. Those in warrior form held weapons. No one took their eyes off our woman.

"Come, Brenna," I ordered. Our beloved hesitated at the mouth of the cave, but then stepped boldly into the clearing. She wore a simple white shift and her silver torc. Her hair was braided and her feet were bare.

The wolves stared at her, eyes shining gold and predatory in the morning light. Her head started to drift up to face her audience. I quickly shoved it down. "Eyes."

I heard a frustrated huff of breath before she obeyed.

We'd walked halfway across the clearing before Siebold stepped in our path.

"Do you see her insolence? Your woman is unruly. She does not know her place in the pack." The Viking faced Samuel, who sat on the far side of the clearing on the great stone he used as a throne. "An Alpha who cannot control one woman is weak."

Samuel stood and stretched, rolling his neck and cracking bone. His muscles worked in his shoulders. He finished by tossing his gold mane back. He looked anything but weak. He ignored the belligerent warrior. Every word, every movement we'd crafted like a ritual, a dance. A display of Samuel's power.

"Is this true, Daegan? Did our woman challenge Siebold for dominance? Even though she is weaker than him, and wouldn't survive a fair fight?"

"She looked him in the eye, Alpha, and struck him." I smirked a little. Siebold couldn't be proud of taking a blow from such a slight adversary. Sure enough he flushed, and snapped his teeth in annoyance.

"She challenged me. Let her fight, or submit to formal punishment."

Samuel beckoned, and Siebold stepped aside. I brought Brenna to the Alpha's side. He wound her braid around his wrist, leashing her. "Poor little love, weakest in the pack."

"She knew the rules," Siebold muttered. "She stepped out of line."

"Perhaps. Or perhaps she knew we protected her." Samuel stared the Viking down. "To challenge her is to challenge us."

"That's right, Siebold," I taunted. "Do ye want to go in the pit and fight him?"

"If you win you would be Alpha." Samuel had planned

this beforehand. If Siebold was making a play for dominance over him, he wanted to know. We would make Siebold admit it.

For a few tense seconds it seemed Siebold would challenge for Alpha. But the bully backed down. "I do not wish to be Alpha," he sneered. The whole pack could smell the lie in his scent. "But rules are rules. If you cannot control your woman and tame her, perhaps you should give her to me."

Samuel's roar cut off my snarl. "Think carefully before you challenge for our woman. To become Alpha, you need only challenge me. To take her, you have to defeat both Daegan and me."

"And me," Wulfgar added, and Fergus echoed the same sentiment. The little wolf wasn't dominant to Siebold, but he'd made it clear that he would fight for our woman all the same.

"Stand down, Viking," Wulfgar ordered.

Siebold's gaze sank to the ground, and for a moment I thought Samuel's plan had worked. We'd placated the stupid warrior. A quick punishment for our woman, and all would be well.

I should've known better. As Siebold slunk away, he said, "Next time we deliver meat to her sisters, I will sample one of them."

Brenna's head snapped up and she flew at the Viking before Samuel or I could stop her.

"Brenna," my voice cracked across the clearing, but it was too late She snatched up a stick, a thick tree branch that lay near the bonfire for kindling, and went after Siebold.

Shock made him pause, and saved Brenna's life. The large blond hunched and growled, his wolf coming over him.

It was over in a flash, but I'd never forget the bone-chilling sight of my mate facing the large golden animal with nothing but her anger and a stick.

Wulfgar's hand clasped on Siebold's scruff, and hauled him back. I caught Brenna and pulled her to my side.

"Kneel," I ordered her furiously, and forced her down. I kept a hand on her head, as a reminder to lower her gaze. I could only imagine her furious expression, but she stayed down, a picture of submission, at least. I hoped it would be enough to placate the pack.

The warriors all waited to see what their Alpha would do. Disobedience like that couldn't go unchecked. The rules were in place to keep the Berserkers from tearing each other apart.

I cursed under my breath.

You see, Siebold whined through the pack bonds. *You see, Alpha?*

"I do see. Brenna."

Brenna flinched under my hand, but didn't look up.

"You must trust your mates to defend you. You are the weakest among us and cannot fight for dominance. You will be punished in front of the pack to learn your place."

A slight slump of her shoulders told me she understood. I warred between wanting to comfort her and wanting to set her over my knee and blister her behind in view of everyone.

Siebold whined happily. Wulfgar yanked him back as if he were a naughty pup.

"Siebold," Samuel addressed the golden wolf. "You will not touch her sisters. We promised we would keep them safe."

"Why not, Alpha?" a warrior asked. "They are so young,

and ripe for the taking. Why do we suffer when these women might help us?"

Another warrior added, "We could just take one...the eldest. The blonde. She will be enough to warm us all through the winter."

A grunt from Siebold, who'd changed back into man form and prowled forward, keeping the fire between us. "I know the blonde. Sweet bitch, she bathes naked in the forest stream. Flaunting herself in front of us...she's practically asking for it."

This time, I noted how Siebold directed his taunts, and kept a hand on Brenna. It didn't matter. With a swift motion, she leaned forward, grabbed up the great stick, and thrust it into the fire.

Not just into the fire—at the cooking pot. The tripod shuddered and the pot tipped, spilling broth onto the hissing fire. Steam rose as the pot rolled towards the scowling Siebold. The warrior leapt out of the way, but not fast enough to escape the hot liquid. He yowled.

This time I hauled our beloved out of the clearing, away from the pack. "Are ye mad, lass?" I'd never guess, in a hundred years, that our woman would behave as she did. It seemed her sweet submissive self went only so far as our chambers.

This was serious. Siebold was mad enough to shift and try to destroy her. Already Wulfgar and Fergus were pushing through warriors to stand between me and the Viking. The wolves were restless, shifting, whining, wondering if there would be a fight.

A sound rolled across the clearing that I didn't expect. Seated on his throne, Samuel was laughing. His chuckle echoed over the clearing. Wulfgar laughed too, and Siebold turned on the great warrior with fury.

"Change," Samuel ordered. Siebold's body jerked from man to beast, forced to obey the Alpha's command. Shrieking human turned into whimpering wolf, easily subdued by Wulfgar and a few others. One or two other wolves in the pack were caught unawares by the Alpha's command and shifted into their animal form. They shuffled out of sight, ashamed. The rest of the pack quieted, on edge, waiting at the Alpha's word.

"We will not touch our woman's sisters. We promised," Samuel said. "Brenna will be punished in front of the pack in lieu of challenging Siebold for dominance. Any challenge she gives will be met with punishment. She's a female and human besides and much weaker." Samuel nodded to me. "Daegan will carry out her discipline for all to see. She is our mate, and our responsibility."

A ripple of energy ran through the pack at the word 'mate.' For a moment, everything on the mountain held its breath.

Yes, said my wolf. *Our mate.*

For once I didn't have the heart to correct it.

"Will she one day bear you pups?" one of the warriors asked.

Samuel's face hardened. "No. But she is our mate none-theless." He motioned to me. "Daegan."

I growled in Brenna's ear as I marched her across the clearing. "That was verra dangerous. I'd almost be proud if I didn't have to punish ye. But now I intend to blister yer backside. Ye earned it."

I handed her over to the Alpha.

"Naughty one," Samuel said. "Now you'll be disciplined like a wolf, stripped bare for all to see."

Fear finally crossed her features. I petted her hair.

"Dinnae worry. It'll hurt, but we'll not let any true harm come to ye. Do ye trust us?"

Fear receded. She met my gaze with clear brown eyes as she nodded.

Samuel helped her kneel at his side. The ritual we'd painstakingly planned would continue. The Alpha looked stern on his throne, in control, but his hand was gentle as he stroked her hair.

Grinning, I loped off, motioning to the small redhead wolf waiting at the mouth of the cave.

"Fergus," I ordered, "fetch me the flogger."

He returned, and I noticed how he was walking with a bit of a swagger. The little wolf had enjoyed watching Siebold humbled by a mere human.

"Dinnae get any ideas," I warned him as he presented the flogger to me. "Otherwise you'll be the one bared to the lash."

I'd spent the past few days practicing for this moment, including an afternoon in a secluded grove, working out my whipping arm with Fergus' back as a target. Samuel and I had planned every moment of this discipline ritual.

Fergus had created this punishment tool. He'd bound soft strips of deerskin into a handle. The strips were soft and supple. Wielded correctly, it would not mar or mark our woman's flesh, though it would sting. I felt a heady rush of arousal at the thought of Brenna's white back bare and lovely, exposed to the flogger's soft kiss. Perhaps, if I handled it well today, she would allow me to use the tool on her in private.

I reached for the implement, but Fergus held it back. "Beta," he said in a quiet, nervous voice. "Ye do not have to do this. Siebold is just trying to pick a fight. The pack will understand." He kept his gaze carefully lowered.

"Not after her stunt, they won't." I stepped closer. "This will not hurt her. Ye helped me make sure of it. Truly, Fergus. I would never cause her undue harm."

My reassurance relaxed him. He looked serious, but the worry lines disappeared from his youthful face.

I stalked to the center of the pack, my eyes on Brenna. Excitement buzzed down the pack bond. The wolves waited, hungry with anticipation.

I motioned and Wulfgar and Fergus—the two warriors we trusted most--crossed to Brenna to pull her up.

She resisted, but at Samuel's warning allowed them to set her on her feet and guide her to a wooden frame we used as a drying rack. The warriors tied Brenna's arms above her head, using leather ties. She faced away from the pack, so they could see the lash hit her back and count each stripe, red on white.

At my nod, Fergus took her braid and placed it over her shoulder, out of the way.

"It'll be all right," I heard Fergus whisper to Brenna.

Wulfgar frowned at the little red wolf, but as soon as Fergus couldn't see his face, he grinned. The giant warrior had a soft spot for smaller beings with undiminished spirit.

Wulfgar stepped away. I took my place in front of the pack. It was so quiet I could hear flies buzzing, and the frightened pants of the bound woman.

It shouldn't excite me but it did.

"Brenna of the Berserker clan, you're being punished for challenging a warrior. This whipping will teach you your place. Pack rules allow you to submit this way instead of fighting to the death."

I prayed she heard these words and understood the gravity of her offense. Berserkers lived and died by the rules, carefully crafted to keep the beast at bay.

It was up to me to complete the ritual. Besides my somber expression, I wore deerskin breeches. My chest was bare. I drew a knife and walked around to face our beloved. I held her eyes as I lifted the blade. She didn't look away, but stayed brave as I cut off her meager shift. The cloth fell and bared her perfect body to every man and wolf in the clearing.

A short whine rose from one, and ended when Samuel growled. Today, the pack could look upon our woman, but we would not let them forget she belonged to us.

Brenna closed her eyes. Her pure skin pebbled, from both the cool mountain air and her own fearful anticipation. I broke the ritual then, leaning forward to kiss her. "Trust me, lass," I breathed against her mouth. She nodded. I caught the slight scent of her musk when I stepped back.

My own cock was painfully hard as I stalked back around and readied the flogger. I snapped it several times before laying it on her back.

I heard a harsh sound as she sucked in a breath, but she relaxed when she realized the impact didn't hurt. I whipped her carefully, painting her upper back and curved buttocks red. These first strikes served to warm her skin and ready it for a long beating. Over time the sting would rise from the striped skin, but for now it would feel as gentle as a massage.

I paused when her skin grew flushed. Brenna's breathing was deep and even. If I could, I would stop here, give her pleasure. But the pack expected her misery.

Flicking my wrist, I let the flogger fly. Brenna's body jerked as the strands hit her with more force. A bright red slash appeared on her skin. Her feet danced as she tried to escape the pain.

Several wolves cheered. Samuel growled again, and silenced them.

I gave Brenna several light strokes before intensifying the blows. Red blossomed on her back, and though I was careful not to let the strands wrap around her front, a few times she twisted and the flogger bit her sides. That would hurt the worst, I knew. The end of the strands felt like bee stings.

The flogging would hurt worse than a spanking, but the marks would fade by the next day. It was nothing like a beating with a true whip made with braided rope, and rocks and pottery shards that could strip a man's flesh.

If I beat her long and gently enough, she might even fall asleep.

I leaned into the rhythm, ignoring the blood pounding in my head and cock. I don't know how long I spent striking her with the flogger. At times I was slow and gentle, alternating with more forceful blows.

I don't know when Brenna stopped fighting and surrendered to the sensation, but as the beating continued, intensified, she didn't flinch. Her head dipped lower and lower, and her whole body went limp. The flogger licked again and again at her soft skin, and a blush spread over her upper back and bottom. I kept whipping her, even as the deep pink turned red.

In the haze of my arousal, I barely heard my Alpha speak.

"Daegan, that's enough."

As soon as I undid her wrists, Brenna slumped against me, huddling under my arms, hiding her face in my chest. The real punishment wasn't the flogging, it was the humiliation. The act of being bared and punished before the pack broke the most belligerent wolf's spirit.

It was necessary. I would tell her, over and over again. I would carry her to our cave and use every unguent I had to soothe her. I would bathe her carefully and kiss away her tears.

Brenna shifted in my arms and I caught a glimpse of her face, the high color in her pale cheeks. There were a few tearstains, but not many.

I sniffed the air and realized what my body and every wolf had picked up on—the sweet, heady musk filling the clearing, lying thick on the summer air.

Our beloved was aroused.

Incredulous, I pushed a fallen strand of hair away from her face. Her eyes were glazed, her expression lax with submission. She breathed against me, her body melting into mine, pliant. She was ready to be taken and fucked, dominated completely.

A hungry whine rose from the ranks of wolves, and this time, no growl from the Alpha could quell it.

"Wulfgar," Samuel called to complete the ritual. "Is the pack satisfied with this punishment?"

"The pack is satisfied," the warrior rumbled.

Daegan, get her inside.

I pulled Brenna past the wolves, eager to hide her away from prying eyes. Behind me, Fergus and Wulfgar followed close, protected our flank from the slavering beasts. As soon as we hit the mouth of the cave I scooped our beloved into my arms. I carried her, careful of her reddened flesh.

In our chambers, I laid our woman down to inspect her back. The strokes had heated her flesh, but none of the strands had broken the skin. She writhed under the lightest touch, and the heady scent of her arousal filled the air. I checked between her legs.

"By the moon, ye are so wet for me." I teased her gently,

stoking the flame lit by the pain in her back. She arched into my hand, ready for me. My fingers thrummed faster between her legs. My other hand reached under her to find a nipple, and pinch it. Her body convulsed.

"That's it, wee love. Take yer pleasure."

I leaned over her, watching her twitch and surrender to the movement of my hand. At the last second, I draped myself over her, pressing my body against her sensitized skin. Her pain melded with pleasure, overwhelming her senses, and she almost bucked me off as her orgasm took her. My cock swelled painfully in my leather breeches. I lifted off her and latched my mouth to the back of her neck, sucking hard enough to leave a red mark.

Mine.

Teeth grew in my mouth, and the wolf yipped with glee at the thought of marking her.

Our woman. Ours.

I snapped my head back, pushing away from her, off the dais, to the other side of the room where it was safe.

She would not survive a mating bite. Tender human skin crushed under a wolf's jaws—how was that love?

The red marks I'd placed on her skin only made me want to mark her permanently.

When I felt calm enough to approach, I got our beloved a drink of water, and held the cup to her lips. Once she drank, I lay beside her, stroking her cheek, kissing her yielding lips.

"Daegan," Samuel entered, and I stood aside at his request.

He knelt and touched her hair, waiting until she roused a little.

"Stay on your belly," he ordered, and examined the marks on her back.

"No blood," I offered.

"She did well," Samuel said and stepped away. I could scent his excitement, but like me, he strolled around the room until he had it under control. "I set a guard at the mouth of the cave, and sent most of the pack on patrol, away from the mountain."

"Just as well. We can fuck her senseless without fear of interruption." I shucked off my pants.

"Brenna," Samuel called, seating himself on a rock. "Come here."

It took her a moment to arrange her limbs so she could walk from the bed, but she made it to the Alpha and stood between his legs so he could steady her.

"You understand why you were punished?"

She nodded.

Samuel stroked back her hair. "It is necessary, little love. Each of us has our place in the pack. Our very survival depends on it.

"You cannot fight a wolf as a challenger is meant to. If you challenge another and cannot follow through, the rules decree you must be punished. It is a mercy that Siebold wasn't allowed to punish you."

Her eyes widened.

Samuel picked up the flogger, examining the soft leather strips and showing our beloved. "Daegan fashioned this for you so you would not be hurt. You will thank him later." He tossed the flogger aside, and his face hardened.

"Kneel," he ordered, she sank down. Samuel spread his legs and brushed aside his loin cloth. Even seated, the Alpha looked powerful, with thick legs and a muscled chest.

"You took your punishment well, little love. And now you will show your Alpha you understand your place."

His hand guided her head to his cock and she sucked it down.

Samuel continued, stroking her hair. "The way of the wolf is hard. We live on the brink of life or death. As Alpha, I protect my pack. I would die for it. The weakest wolves are to be protected. But I cannot do this if they disobey my commands. The slightest hesitation could mean the difference between life or death."

He sucked in a breath as Brenna bobbed her head, sliding several inches down his cock before coming off with a pop. Her tongue lapped lazily over him.

My own balls tightened in sympathy.

"All the way down now," the Alpha ordered, and, with a deep breath, Brenna obeyed.

"Good girl. Take it all."

Samuel made her work on her knees until he grunted and spent himself in her mouth.

Brenna bobbed her head leisurely until Samuel gripped her hair and pulled it off with a plop. He bent her head back so her eyes met his.

"The next time you put yourself in danger, attacking a warrior like that, I will have Daegan whip you with more than just a soft flogger. And more than once. You won't sleep on your back for weeks. Do you understand?"

Brenna nodded, lips soft and shining.

"She's all yours," Samuel said to me, stern expression falling away.

"Here, Brenna," I ordered. "Crawl up on the dais. Hands and knees."

She slunk gracefully towards me, and I nearly spent myself at the sight.

As she passed, I caught her chin. Her eyes were half

lidded with pleasure. I touched her lip and she licked my finger in a submissive haze.

"Ye are all right, lass," I chuckled and helped her onto the pelt covered rock. "Now arch yer back and present yer lovely arse to me."

She did as I commanded, her breathing coming harsher with excitement.

She expected a good hard fucking, and that's exactly what she was going to get. I picked up the jar of oil and coated my fingers before spreading it liberally over the crevice between her reddened bottom cheeks.

She sucked in a breath, tensing and pulling away. I smacked the side of her hip. "No, arse up. Naughty lassies get their bottoms fucked hard."

Happy haze gone, she struggled and tried to crawl away. I gripped her hips and pulled her back.

Samuel came to crouch in front of her, lifting her hair from her face and speaking softly,

"You've done so well," he crooned. "You know we'd never truly hurt you, right? But this is ours to claim."

He glanced up at me and I nodded, continuing to spread oil on my own cock, and smear it over her tiny pucker. "You've taken the plug just fine. Daegan is using plenty of oil on you and himself. He'll slide right in. It'll be tight, but we'll make sure it feels good. And we'll love taking you there. You want to please us, don't you?" His hand slipped under her, playing with her breast. She arched her back further, pushing into his hand and presenting her lovely bottom to me at the same time.

Ready, I set my cock at her rear entrance, admiring the sight of me against her pink cheeks, mottled with the marks I'd given her.

"I'm going to take ye now, Brenna. And one day, Samuel and I will both claim ye."

Gripping her arse cheeks, I held them apart as I pushed in, waiting until she relaxed to inch forward. My own breathing grew labored as more of her sweet flesh swallowed my cock.

"Och, you're a grand sight." I squeezed her hip and she shuddered and clenched around my member, I gasped and saw stars. Samuel chuckled at the string of happy curses that fell from my lips.

"Time for yer reward," I slowed my thrusts. Leaning over her flushed back, I reached under and played with her slippery lower lips, finding the little hard nub and circling it gently.

Brenna squirmed, but Samuel and I held her in thrall, forcing her to take her pleasure with my cock in her ass. She didn't struggle very long. All the sting and heat combined to make her one very aroused woman.

Her arsehole fluttered around my cock, almost squeezing the life out of me. My mind soared, but I grabbed her braid, using it as a leash to pull her back on me.

"This is how we'll fuck ye, whenever you disobey. Naughty lass," I tugged her hair and heard her gasp. The squelching around my cock told me she was more aroused than subdued. "Ye won't mind our commands? Verra well. We'll fuck ye into submission, and tie ye up so ye can never leave."

"How is it?" Samuel asked. "Tight?"

"Any tighter and she'll snap off my cock."

"Think she can take faster?"

"Only one way to find out. She'll take whatever we give her, and more." I tugged her braid, pulling her head back. "Won't ye lass? Ye forget yer place, we'll remind you." I sped up, scything in and out of her. "Yer place is on yer knees, taking our cocks."

I guided her up, holding her so I could bounce her up and down as fast as I wanted her to go. She reached back and hung on to my shoulder as I thrust up into her, again and again. Samuel knelt before her, plucking her nipples.

"Soon you'll take both of us," he promised her. "One in your cunt and one in your ass."

"Would ye like that, Brenna?" I asked.

Her orgasm rocked her body. I climaxed with her, gripping her tight. My teeth found her shoulder and bit down gently. From the way her body shuddered, I knew her pleasure went on and on.

TWO DAYS LATER, I walked down the mountain path at the end of my patrol. A group of wolves stood around the fire, waiting for a giant boar to finish roasting.

My ears pricked up at the sound of Siebold's voice.

"Stupid cur."

I came around the rock to see what was going on. Siebold had his hands around Fergus' throat.

"Siebold, let him go."

The warrior growled but released the little red wolf, who gasped and wriggled away. "Why? You want to fuck him? Your woman doesn't satisfy you?"

I ignored the Viking's taunts.

"Admit it. Your beast isn't satisfied with sex without pain. It wants to mark her. The flogging just gave it a taste of what could be--"

"Let it go, Siebold."

He fell silent, and I started to walk away when I heard

him comment to another warrior, "Now if I had that dumb bitch I would do what it took to make her scream—"

I cleared the space between us in a second. I leaped and my body hit his, sending him staggering. The blond Viking was broader and taller than I was, but I was quicker.

Warriors scrambled out of our way, pulling away the logs they used as seats to give us room to fight.

The beast clamored to break free and I let it. My spine cracked with the Change. Hands turned to claws.

Siebold shifted, half beast himself, his features contorting and elongating into something between a human jaw and a wolf's maw. In a second, he was sprinting my way. He leapt and I fell to my back, kicking his body when it would land on mine, sending him feet over head away from me. I bounded up and faced him just in time for him to make another pass.

Teeth like blades snapped close to my face. I saw an opening, and raked my claws across his back. He bellowed, arching backwards. Before he could turn and face me, I tackled him, driving him to the ground.

I wanted him to hurt.

Gripping his blond hair, I ground Siebold's face into the dirt. He was too pretty. I could fix that.

The beast within fought for dominance. My world started to turn black, void of all color but the red pooling on the dirt in front of Siebold...

"Daegan, enough." Samuel ordered. I felt a whisper of my Alpha's magic wash over me, and jerked up to my feet, away from Siebold. Anything to avoid the humiliation of being forced to shift into full wolf.

Siebold made snuffling noises as he tried to rise. With a snap of my jaws, I roared at him to stay put. He flattened himself against the ground, pleasing the beast enough for me to gain the upper hand.

Claws like knives sprouted from my fur clad fingers. My stomach lurched, sick with self-disgust.

I stalked past Samuel, into the cave to find our beloved.

She wanted to stay as our consort? I'd show her the monster I really was.

I found her in the garden. My snuffling grunts alerted her. She looked up and went white. Rising, she paced to the far side of the chamber, setting her back to the wall and taking a deep breath before she looked me in the eye.

I knew what she saw—black fur, a man's standing form, a beast's paws. I was neither man nor wolf, but a creature of nightmares, with Siebold's blood dripping from my claws.

The pulse fluttered in her throat as she took in my misshapen form, and fought her fear. She didn't run—there was nowhere for her to go. She didn't scream because she could not.

The hair on the back of my neck prickled. Samuel spoke from behind me.

"Let me help you, Daegan."

I whined, a brutal, broken sound.

Brenna's fear fell away, replaced by pity. I hunched over, paws covering my face, and felt Samuel's order waft over my body, straightening my spine. Muscle and bone responded, fur disappeared. I stood a man, but I kept a hand over my face until I felt our woman's gentle touch. Brenna tugged my hands down and cupped my face with her own. Nothing but acceptance shone in her eyes. She sealed it with a kiss.

At the touch of her lips, the last of the Berserker rage fell away.

"Come, Brenna," Samuel said in a rough voice. "It's time for you to understand what we truly are."

I let her lead me into our bed chamber. We lay together on the dais with Brenna between us. I held her lush body, while Samuel faced her.

"The magic gives us many things," Samuel told Brenna. "Longer life, the ability to fight, to heal. But the beast lurks forever in our mind, waiting to take hold and drive out our reason. That is the gift, and the curse."

She glanced back at me. I nodded. My speech was slow returning from the beast's grip. Any sound I made would be an animal's grunt. I was too ashamed to utter it.

"We thought we were doomed, until the witch told us of you. We have no right to ask you to stay, but we do."

"You should leave us, lass," I said. "The beast takes over quickly. If we ever lost control—"

"If I ever lost control," Samuel corrected. "For it is likely to be me." He touched Brenna. "If that happens, Daegan has orders to send you away."

She frowned and shook her head.

"Yes," I captured her face in my palms. "It is for the best. You will live a long life without us."

She pointed to each of us and then to her heart.

"We love you too, beloved," Samuel said. "And as long as you love us, we will always be with you."

The moon waxed as we settled into the hottest month of the year. A weight lifted off me, now that Brenna had seen my Berserker form, and knew if Samuel ever lost control, she must run.

Our plan to accept her as one of the pack continued as we allowed her time off the mountain. Together we enjoyed the spoils of summer.

One afternoon, I was speaking with Wulfgar at the firepit when Fergus rushed up with the first horn of mead.

I tasted it and found it good. Wulfgar agreed with me.

"Bring a barrel of that to the Thing," he advised. "A good mead goes a long way to soothing tempers."

"Any more word from the Red Pack?"

"They complain Berserkers are on their land."

"Siebold?" The blond Viking had made himself scarce since Brenna had baptized him in meat broth. After our fight, I expected to hear he'd been holed up with a village woman or three, until his beast broke free and needed someone to clean up the mess.

Wulfgar shook his head. "Not our pack. Ragnvald's. They

complain of the new pack. They seem to think it's our duty to rein in Ragnvald's warriors. That is why they want Samuel at the gathering. They think he will be willing to take over this second Berserker pack."

I scoffed. "The Red Pack is so spineless, they want us to do their dirty work for them."

"They hate us," Wulfgar stated.

"They hate the taint. They hope we will fight Ragnvald's Berserkers, and wipe them out. Or they do the same to us."

"Perhaps we should make peace with Ragnvald."

"A little late for that. His second wastes away in our pit."

Wulfgar didn't try to argue that we should let Maddox go. It made sense to use the tattooed wolf as a bargaining chip, but he couldn't be allowed to live. He knew too much. Letting him go would put Brenna at risk.

Wulfgar tossed the rest of the mead back, and started to hand the horn to Fergus, who'd listened to our political chatter with wide eyes and sharp ears. A raven landed on Wulfgar's outstretched arm, and let out a squawk.

"Thor's balls," Wulfgar ducked and swore. The raven disappeared in a puff of smoke, and we all ducked and swore with him.

"What sorcery is this?" Fergus pointed to the place the bird had been. Beneath the smoke lay a scrap of birch bark, with black marks scrawled on the white surface. I crouched and picked it up.

"Damn witch." After ordering Wulfgar to be on the lookout for Yseult, I trotted the message to Samuel. During his time as a monk, he'd learned to read.

"She's coming to visit by the full moon."

"Does she know more about our true mate?"

Samuel shook his head. "My guess is she has some information for us. She's sending an emissary ahead of her. We should expect him soon."

The next day, an old man climbed the mountain. Berserkers dogged his steps, but didn't stop him until he reached our fire, and stood before Samuel, who lounged on a great rock in a loincloth, looking like a barbarian king on his throne.

The old man had a long, grey beard and a cloth wrapped around his head, covering his right eye. Samuel stared at him a long time before nodding to me.

"Who are ye?" I asked for Samuel.

"Yseult calls me Odin. Like him, I gave an eye for wisdom."

The Viking wolves who were watching grew unsettled. They were likely to believe a blind old man called Odin really was their god.

I rolled my eyes. Yseult playing tricks again.

"What is your business here?"

The man spread his hands. "Yseult bade me come. She said you would give me food and shelter, in return for my services."

"What services does a blind, old man offer?"

The greybeard smiled and spread his hands. "I am going to teach your beloved to speak."

IT TOOK another night and day before we allowed the old man near Brenna. She approached curiously, stopping when I caught her arm.

"Hello, Brenna," Odin said, using his hands to make symbols in the air. He repeated his greeting, motioning slower.

Samuel and I watched in fascination as she mimicked his gestures. After greetings, the greybeard pointed to things in the room, naming them out loud and with a gesture.

After a few days, she'd mastered this new game. Samuel and I practiced along with her, but we learned more slowly.

"Did you speak like this with anyone?" greybeard asked.

Yes. My sister, she signed back. *The one closest to me in age.*

"Sabine?" I asked. I knew her sisters' names from reports of the wolves who checked on them from time to time.

Brenna looked at the floor, as she always did when we spoke of her family. *Yes.*

"Leave us," Samuel ordered the greybeard. Wisely, the man called Odin obeyed.

"Brenna," I crouched near her, to meet her gaze. "Do ye miss yer sisters?"

Yes.

"Do ye wish to see them?"

A pause, then she shook her head. *It is easier if I don't.*

Samuel and I exchanged glances.

"Do ye wish to leave us?"

Her gaze jerked up at that. *No,* she indicated, and I felt relief. But she didn't leave it at that. *I would miss you more.*

With a growl, Samuel crossed to her. Tugging her head back by her braid, he claimed her lips. "Then you are ours, lass. Forever."

10

I was standing at the fire when the Yseult appeared beside me. Even though we'd had guards posted for days, on the lookout for the blonde woman, she'd cloaked herself to show her power, coming close to our beloved without warning, without asking permission.

I smelled her awful scent, cold smoke and stone, and kept my eyes on the fire. "I hate it when ye appear out of thin air."

"I know you do." She smiled. "Did you enjoy my little gift?"

"The old man? He knows some tricks."

My flesh crawled as she studied me. "Has she bonded with you?"

"She speaks with us, using the language of the hands," I hedged.

"Take me to her."

I led her inside. Brenna sat with the old man beside the pool, their hands flashing as they spoke with gestures.

I stopped in the entryway and threw out my arm to keep Yseult back.

The witch obeyed my silent command. Together we watched Brenna converse silently. She didn't notice us, but Samuel did. The Alpha prowled closer.

"Well, Yseult? What do you think of our mate?"

"Is that what she is? Your mate?"

"Yes. We do not care what the runes say. She is the one we choose."

"Hmm," Yseult made a noncommittal noise. "Her scent is different. Stronger. You awakened something within her."

"What do you mean? Speak plainly, or not at all." Samuel ordered.

"She smells like she is in heat. Her body responds to the pull of your magic."

"Explain."

"When I last visited, you promised me a night with the pack. During the summer solstice. That is today."

"The pack is ready for you. We will uphold our end of the bargain. Now tell us why Brenna smells like she is in heat."

"And why she survived the dog attack when she was young," I added.

Yseult smiled her damned enigmatic smile. She loved lording over us. "Brenna has magic."

"Witch?"

"She's not a witch. Not quite. Hers is a more subtle, earthy magic." Yseult sniffed, and we knew she felt Brenna was beneath her. "Your Brenna is a hedgewitch, like her mother, and her mother's mother. Also called a spaewife. They are less powerful than witches."

"But she has some power? What is it?"

"That you must find out. I searched for the answer and learned of Brenna's grandmother, who had some healing abilities. Not much power, at least, not enough to keep the villagers from burning her alive."

"What about Brenna's mother?"

"After the grandmother's death, the mother took her children and fled. If she has any power, it deserted her when she took to the drink. What powers a spaewife has, Brenna and her sisters have the answer."

Samuel and I exchanged glances. Whatever we thought the witch knew, we hadn't expected this. "This is all you discovered? Our woman is a spaewife, perhaps with healing powers?"

"It makes sense," I added. "She soothes the beast."

"But she has not fully tamed it," Samuel said.

Yseult cleared her throat. "Power grows with sacrifice. There is always a price."

"What's Brenna's price? She already lost her voice, almost her life."

"The same price we all pay," Yseult said. "Pain."

BY EVENING, all the pack had assembled around the fire pit on the mountain. Samuel sat on his throne. Yseult stood to the side, wearing a white shift and an enigmatic smile.

By Yseult's request, I stood with Brenna at the mouth of the cave, a safe distance from the pack. We would watch, and learn.

Pain. The witch had said. I knew that witches like my mother and Yseult sacrificed for magic. The sacrifice could be small—a rabbit or a dove. Or personal—like Odin, who gave his eye for wisdom. Or something else...like surrendering to an erotic beating. I wondered if the flogging had awakened Brenna's powers.

Brenna and I waited as Samuel gave his orders to the pack. For one night, they could take Yseult and use her as they would. No maiming or death. Those were the only rules.

When Samuel finished, Yseult descended into the pack of wolves, her eyes alight with a primal hunger. She walked through the warriors until one stepped in her path. A wicked smile curved her lips. She spoke to Siebold. Then her hand flashed out and slapped him across the face.

No one breathed.

Siebold's eyes glowed gold with the beast as he reached out and gripped her hair. He dragged her head back and kissed her.

Three other warriors closed around her, ripping the shift off her tall form. Siebold lifted and carried her to the ground, already rutting.

Yseult's teeth found his neck and bit down. Blood flowed, and Siebold roared, pounding her into the ground with his hips as her nails raked down his back.

When she orgasmed, magic whipped through the pack. All the wolves howled. All but Samuel and I.

"Come, Brenna." I started to turn away, sickened not by the display, but by my cock's reaction to it. Brenna stopped me, tugging on my arm.

"What is it, lass?" My mouth dried as I saw the heat in our beloved's eyes. She hooked an arm around my neck and brought me down into a searing kiss.

I almost staggered back when she let me go. "Really? Now?"

She nodded, her hand on my chest. I wasted no time throwing her up over my shoulder, and carrying her to our bed chambers.

BRENNA TREMBLED when I set her down on the dais.

"Are ye all right, lass?"

Yes. Her hands fluttered. *Need. You. Now.*

Samuel bounded into the chamber, looking younger and more carefree than I'd seen him in a long time.

"I can smell her," he said, his eyes swimming with gold. His beast was close to the surface, I could smell it, but it did not seem angry.

"Brenna," the big Alpha choked out. "You're in heat." He came to stand before her on the dais, running his hand down her breasts to her cunny. She pressed into his touch, her eyes fluttering.

"Your heat calls to us. It is intoxicating." He pressed his face to her stomach through the gown, looking like a supplicant before a queen. "I will do whatever you ask."

She looked thoughtful, then a wicked smile crossed her face and she pointed to the ground in front her.

"You want me to please you, little love? You want your Alpha on his knees?" He sank down before Brenna, his head coming to her knees as she stood on the dais. Pushing aside her gown, he lifted one foot, then the other, nibbling at her ankles and moving up. Grabbing his hair to steady herself, Brenna pulled him between her legs.

I bounded up onto the dais and raised her gown, pulling it over her head. Earlier that day, I'd shaved and plugged her. Her body was smooth and ready. I kissed her neck.

"You are the only one, Brenna. The only one we kneel for."

I lifted her and Samuel draped her legs over his shoulders. Brenna sighed and writhed as he nibbled on her folds. I steadied her, freeing one hand to brush her breast. Her head fell back onto my shoulder, but she kept holding Samuel's head to her cunny, even after her orgasm crested.

Samuel and I laid her down, stroking her pale skin as she recovered.

"So fragile. So delicate...and yet you are stronger than us all. Your frailty calls to our beast, turns our brutal beast into a protector."

I drew in a deep breath, realizing it was true. The beast wasn't stronger because we were losing our grip on it. It was stronger because she needed it, wanted it, accepted it.

Samuel put a finger to her lips. "You knew before we did."

Brenna's lips curved against his fingers as she smiled her secret smile. That was when I knew the runes had been right. This was the woman for us.

"Up," I commanded, holding out my hands to help her to her knees. Reaching around her, I slid my hand over her bottom and seized the plug. "Here."

Her eyes widened, but she allowed me to maneuver her to all fours.

We'd plugged her often, stretching her back hole for us. And now we would claim it.

"All of ye belongs to us." I fucked her arse with the plug, sliding it in and out.

Samuel handed me the jar of oil. I pulled out the plug and rimmed her with a finger coated in oil. Brenna lay with her chest to the pelts and her arse waving in the air, ready for us.

"Don't be afraid, lass."

Samuel stepped forward, fisting his cock in readiness. First he pulled her to all fours and plunged into her cunny. I slid under her and lapped at her breasts until her breathing changed from forced to ragged.

Samuel pulled out and prised her arse cheeks apart. "Beautiful."

I held her in my arms as Samuel set his cock against her pucker and started to press in.

Sweat appeared on her brow. She hid her face in my chest.

I stroked her hair.

"Focus on us. Focus on pleasing yer masters." I whispered.

Without raising her head, she nodded.

"Breathe in. Then breathe out and bear down."

Samuels' grunt told me when he'd sheathed himself in her.

"So tight. So fucking tight."

"There now, lass, ye did it. Now," I scooted back so my cock waved in front of her face. "Suck on this."

Her body moved back and forth between us.

We came in unison.

We hadn't taken her cunny and arse together, but soon.

11

The next day, a few hours after dawn, I climbed the mountain to the overlook to take the first watch.

A wind wafted by my face, carrying the scent of snow and cold stone, a touch of death. Yseult.

"Did ye get what ye came for?"

"And more." The woman practically purred. "You didn't join in?" she ran a finger down my arm. I caught her hand, willing myself not to crush it.

"I'm spoken for."

"I see that," she laughed, and touched my shoulder, where I noticed marks from Brenna's nails for the first time. "You survived her first mating heat."

"That was—" I choked out. "It didn't seem real. Or I thought it was a response to yer magic in the pack bonds."

"That was her," Yseult murmured. "The spaewife grows stronger every moon she spends in your care. Be careful, wolf," She shook a finger in my face. "There are werewolves who will smell it too, and try to take her from you."

"Let them come," I growled. "There is none as strong as a Berserker."

"Are you sure?" Her smile was beautiful and terrible at the same time. She walked away, hips swaying like a woman well fucked, until she vanished in a bolt of lightning that left my hair standing on end.

It struck me, then, that Yseult had smelled more powerful than before, more than just a boost she would get from spilling her bedmate's blood. Had she eaten one of the pack? I thought through each member of the pack—all wolves were accounted for.

All but one.

I ran down the mountain. When I came to the place of the pit, I slowed and called out to Maddox.

He did not answer. I sniffed the air, but couldn't make out his scent. I leaned over the pit to look for the body.

There was none.

~

SAMUEL DIDN'T LOOK surprised when I delivered the news of the empty prison. I wondered if a part of him hoped Maddox had escaped.

"The witch could've found a way to consume Maddox and his power," I reminded him. "She seems more powerful."

"We are more powerful. Whatever magic Brenna has, it has strengthened us."

I still worried about the beast taking hold. It responded to Brenna in a way I'd never seen before.

"We will keep taking precautions," Samuel read my worry. "You will travel with a few of the pack to the gathering with the Red Pack. Listen and learn what you can of Ragnvald's Berserkers. I will stay here and keep our mate safe." He smiled, and once again I was struck by how much younger he looked. Like a weight had been lifted from his shoulders. "She is waiting for you in the bathing chamber."

I spent a long while taking my leave. Brenna was especially feisty, slapping my hands away and asking over and over why I had to leave. I told her I was visiting a market to buy her pretty things, and she called me a liar. I told her I was going to say goodbye to the village whores, and she hit me and called me a rabbit. I couldn't let that insult slide, so I stripped her, spanked her and fucked her on the stone floor.

Samuel found us like that, our hands running over each other as we spoke silently about our love.

"The pack is waiting," he finally ordered. "It's time."

It wasn't until the thick woods closed around us, blocking out the sight of our mountain, that my spirits fell. The dread that started with Yseult grew stronger with every step that took me from my beloved. Wulfgar noticed my serious silence.

"What can you tell us about the Red Pack?" he asked, seeking to divert my thoughts and focus me on the battle at hand.

"They've been here since the Romans, maybe before. A few of them ruled as lairds, and though the worship of the White Christ drove them into hiding, they think of themselves as civilized. They're natural werewolves, and shift into wolves whenever they will."

"What's the difference between them and us?" Fergus asked. Samuel ordered the runt of the pack to tag along to learn something of diplomacy.

"Most werewolves are natural born, by a female were. Berserkers are created with tainted magic."

"But you weren't Changed by a witch," the young wolf insisted.

"Nay, lad. I was born to one. My mother was a witch,

much like Yseult. Less powerful, though, which is why she bore me. Most witches are barren." I paused for a moment, wondering if Brenna's magic allowed her to bear children. It would be too much to hope for in this lifetime—a mate who could give us a family. "My mother fell in love with my father, and bore him a son. I can shift, aye, but the magic of my mother adds a taint that leads to the Berserker rage."

"Witches and wolves don't mix," Wulfgar grunted. He'd kept away from Yseult, and made Fergus do the same. "No offense, Beta."

"None taken. My mother's first intent on snaring my father was to make him her slave. In the end, love made her his thrall, and caused her death."

Fergus gulped. "He killed her?"

"No. His pack did."

I picked up the pace and the warriors followed. We wore clothes made of deerskin and carried weapons. Most were-wolves relied on teeth and claws; their human forms were more vulnerable. But we were Berserkers. We had been men once, and changed by tainted magic.

We traveled fast and avoided the places of men.

We arrived at the gathering site, a valley between a fringe of hills. The eerie plain was filled with mist, its center marred only by a circle of stones. As we descended, the air became hard to breathe, as if the veil between the worlds grew thin.

"Is that them?" Fergus asked when men appeared out of the mist. "They're smaller than we are."

I glanced down at him. The smallest of our pack was a head taller than most of these shapes slinking out of the mist. "They look like normal men."

"Normal men, natural wolves," I agreed. "They live in harmony with the earth, and hate witch's magic."

We stood on one side of the hill, waiting for the Red Pack to descend into the place of stones. They wore their clan colors, their hair wild and knives strapped against their boots.

The last time I faced these Highland wolves, they tried to kill me. Samuel had intervened, and fixed the bond between us forever.

"This was your pack, yes?" Wulfgar asked me quietly.

"Aye." I started forward, and he held out a hand.

"Let me."

I nodded and held back. Let them think Wulfgar was our leader until the right moment. If I had my way, we wouldn't meet them as equals at all. As I watched Wulfgar and the others stride to the standing stones, I wished I was leading a sneak attack on the pack that had torn my family apart.

Samuel and I had discussed it. The Red Pack was weaker than us. We could defeat them and be done with it, but that would risk loosing the beast.

Wulfgar and the others met the Red Pack at the standing stones. I slunk closer, muting my power so they couldn't sense me and the energy that would mark me as an Alpha.

Fergus was right. After years living with the Berserkers, the members of the Red Pack seemed shrunken, smaller. I studied the trio of leaders and didn't bother to repress my cold killer sense. The ruddy wolf in the center was the largest. Tear off his head in an impressive show of strength, and the others would scatter.

It would be so easy, the darkest part of me whispered. Kill them all and take their women for the pack.

Ha. A nice fantasy. Female werewolves wanted nothing to do with Berserkers.

I kept my thoughts on our beloved, waiting for me in the bathing chamber, her body embraced by the steam rising off the water. The image kept my beast occupied until I heard Wulfgar answer one of the Red Pack Alphas.

"Samuel is not here. But there is one who speaks for him, one who Samuel claims as a brother. Their thoughts are one, their words are one." Wulfgar stepped aside, and let the Red Pack see me stride out of the mists, into the chilling.

My eyes glowed gold; the beast was close to the surface as I faced the pack who killed my mother, drove out my father, and tried to stone me. I'd grown since then, the power of the Alpha making me stronger, faster, prouder. Or maybe it was the acceptance of my warrior brother and the pack that made me stand taller. And now I had a woman worth fighting for. I could face my one time tormentors.

I grew close enough to hear their worried murmurs.

"Half breed," one of the Red Pack spat.

I growled a warning, echoed in the snarls of the Berserkers. The Red Pack recoiled. There were twice as many of them as us, they'd turned out in full force, trying to deter an attack. My lip curled. A thousand armies couldn't stand before Berserkers, if we chose to fight.

"I taste yer fear, wolf," I said. "Speak quickly, before we grow weary of yer posturing, and decide to gut ye."

One of the Red Pack leaders drew himself up. "There is another pack, a threat to ye."

"Ye mean they are a threat to you. Nothing threatens a Berserker."

"A threat to both of us. After all, what's to stop the Red Pack from allying with these new Berserkers to wipe ye out?"

"Ye like yer head attached to yer shoulders."

"We have a way to keep the peace."

I crossed my arms over my chest. I wasn't going to like this.

"We know ye have a woman."

I shrugged. "We often take whores for our amusement."

"But you've claimed this one." The Red Pack chief continued, "Word is she's more than just a village trollop."

I reached through the pack bonds, setting every wolf on alert.

How do they know? I asked Wulfgar. The big warrior shook his head, a subtle motion.

None of our warriors talked.

"What does this matter?" I feigned nonchalance.

"If there is a woman who...counteracts the taint...she is a rare commodity."

"She is rare. Strong, beautiful, submissive. Willing to accept a Berserker cock—unlike your women," I smiled at one of the female wolves. Her mates closed ranks around her, blocking her from my view.

"Am I to believe this wild tale? That the woman we keep has special powers? She's a good fuck, aye, but she doesn't have a magic cunt. Who told ye all this?"

"I did."

I knew the voice even before I turned to look. There, on the rise, stood a man. He was leaner than I last saw him. The bones of his ribs protruded under the skin marked with blue tattoos.

Maddox.

He took a few steps down the hill, but didn't come any closer. A few of his pack appeared behind him. Most were blond and burly, they could be brothers to Samuel or Siebold. Definitely Viking.

"I visited their mountain, and learned their secret. That is why they condemned me to die." He smiled mirthlessly. "Good thing it isn't easy to kill a Berserker."

"We want to live in peace. If there is a woman who can heal the beast—"

I growled a denial.

"—Then you must share her."

"Never. We've claimed her. She is ours."

"Is she your true mate?" Maddox asked, cocking his head to the side. His words were an echo of Yseult's. I wondered if she had something to do with this.

"She's bonded to us," I lied. "If she leaves us, she will die."

"Impossible. No human can bond with a wolf," said the Red Pack leader.

As he repeated what I had told myself for so long, I realized that it wasn't true. Brenna was special. She was human, but had abilities we could only guess at. For the first time, I felt possibilities before me like an open road.

"If she has not mated with ye," the Red Pack leader intoned, "she will survive a separation."

I focused on the problems at hand. Then I felt the wind shift.

Daegan. Someone cried out for me. Not Samuel, not one of the pack, but a softer voice, one I didn't recognize. I glanced at Maddox and his Berserker guards, and felt my dread increase.

"You will never take her from us," I said, just as I heard the voice cry my name again, in panic.

Daegan!

Maddox smiled and I didn't understand why. What had he done?

"She is ours. Find another to sate your needs," I told him.

"It is not yers to decide," said the Red Pack leader. "We

put it to a vote. And yer vote will be outnumbered, Berserker."

I snarled, and the warriors at my back did the same. I felt the beast grip me, and this time I welcomed it. Something was going on, something I couldn't understand...yet. "Vote all you want. We'll back our claim with teeth and claws. Do you really want to vote with your spilled blood?"

Maddox's Berserkers also growled at us. The Red Pack members looked increasingly uneasy, trapped between two contingents of angry Berserkers.

"You want a fight? We'll give you one," Maddox snapped. "We'll fight for our prize."

"You'll never take her." I was losing my grip on the beast, sliding into the Berserker bloodlust. My vision blurred red.

Wulgar's hand closed on my arm. *Beta. Something's wrong.*

I knew he was right. Maddox and the warriors waited for us to attack. They were waiting...

I leaped back and started running, as if in retreat. It all made sense now. The invitation to the Thing, Maddox sniffing around the mountain, his imprisonment and escape. It was all planned, from the first moment. Maddox was a spy, sent to confirm the rumor of our secrets. This meeting was a diversion, meant to draw our strongest forces away from the vulnerable center, the one person we tried to protect and hide.

Back, back. I ordered. *To the mountain. Samuel is under attack.*

Trees blurred as I ran. The beast came over me and I let it, using the superhuman power to speed along. A hint of red fur flashed ahead of me--Fergus, running ahead of the pack. The little wolf was the fastest of us.

Then another figure came close—a flash of blue on my right. Maddox.

"If we all can't have her, no one will."

I swiped at him, but didn't let him slow me down. If he tried to stop me, I'd rip his limbs off and not break a sweat.

Stupid, stupid. I should've left the thing at the first sight of Maddox. I prayed I wasn't too late.

As I grew closer to home, the voices in the pack bonds grew stronger.

A wave of Berserkers, storming the mountain. From the South. Guards taken by surprise. The main path is blocked.

Samuel, I'm here. I send a message along our private bond.

Daegan, what happened?

Ragnvald planned this. The Thing was a trap. Where are you?

Escaping the mountain by a private tunnel. Brenna's with me —she's safe.

I felt relief at that.

Stay hidden. We arrive by sundown.

I put on another burst of speed, and the pack responded. Berserker rage took over, heightening our sense for one another, as well as our need for violence. The mountain reared up out of the horizon. Pain shot through my limbs, not from exertion, but from pack bonds. Our warrior brothers were fighting, dying. I reached out to Wulfgar.

Split in two. One group flank the attackers. The other to head off our followers.

As the mountain grew closer, I felt him obey me. Fergus and I and two others pressed on, while Wulfgar and the rest stopped to guard our flank. The little red wolf ran before me, tearing up the ground in his angry beast form. I followed him all the way onto our lands, then outran him to reach the foot of the mountain

The first of Ragnvald's men met his death before he even saw me. The giant blond head rolled past me as I turned, claws tipped with blood, to attack the men on the main trail up to the cave. From the howls behind me, Wulfgar and the rest were fighting their own battles.

Samuel? Where?

I tried to reach the Alpha while the beast in me tore into more Berserker flesh. After years holding back, pretending to be just a man, it was a relief to let the monster rule. The enemy was strong, but slow, as if dulled. I wondered how close Ragnvald's pack was to madness, and whether their Alpha was here. Maddox was right—Ragnvald would have to be desperate, insane, to attack us here.

I'm here, Samuel sent the image of the tunnel that would bring him and Brenna to the foot of the mountain.

Stay there. We'll fight them off.

Daegan, he choked out, sending more images, too fast for me to see. Ragnvald's Berserkers, attacking, Samuel secreting Brenna back into the caves. The beast in him tried to break free to deal with the threat. His vision was starting to go red.

Stay hidden, I sent my panicked plea to him. More of Ragnvald's Berserkers poured down the mountain, fighting me. I ducked and parried, taking their blows and returning my own. My skin crisscrossed with a hundred cuts, but I felt nothing except when I hacked down another enemy and lusted for more.

We're at the mouth of the tunnel. Samuel sent me the image. *Brenna is safe.*

Do not attempt to fight, Alpha. It will incite the beast.

A flash of blue went by me, and I dispatched the

slavering monster in front of me to follow. Maddox was the most dangerous of our enemies, full of trickery. Behind me, Ragnvald's Berserkers fell to our warriors, except for those who turned and sprinted after their tattooed Beta.

I ran after them, rounding the mountain, intent on catching Maddox until I realized where he was headed. The pit.

"Samuel," Maddox's roar shook the mountain. "Come face me. Coward—you left me to die. Face me like a warrior."

No, Samuel! I felt the beast within my Alpha raise its monstrous head. It was too late. In the heat of the attack, the beast responded to a challenge. The presence of our enemies, the battle brought to our home, the threat to our beloved was enough to snap Samuel's careful control, and send his bloodlust roaring through him, and the entire pack. Before sanity was lost, I sent a final, desperate message. *Leave Brenna, run!*

A roar shook the mountain. Maddox stopped in his tracks and his warriors stopped with him. I rushed him, hoping to tear my claws into his flesh. He turned, a crazy light in his eyes.

"It's over, Beta. You lose."

Before I could touch him, he dodged. I stopped, refusing to chase him. Brenna was in the tunnel with a raging Samuel. I had to protect her.

Before I could race to her, another roar rang out, tinged with tainted magic. I dropped flat on my belly, shivering. The beast within struggled, wild to break away from my control. Tainted magic rushed through the pack bonds, dragging many of the pack under. I felt them succumb, turn into slavering beasts with no thought but destruction.

That was when the tide of the battle turned, and

Maddox's forces retreated, or lost their lives. Not all of them were fast enough to escape the raging beast that used to be Samuel. Gold fur covered his misshapen body, his eyes turned red with the beast bloodlust, he savaged the few straggling enemies.

I dragged myself over the grass until I could sneak into the tunnel. Brenna sat there, curled into a ball, quivering.

"It's all right, lass," I hissed when she shied away from me. I knew I looked like a monster, my body half man, half wolf. But the beast hadn't quite taken hold. I shuttered my mind against the madness swirling down the pack bonds. "We have to go. It's over. Samuel has lost control. He'll rage until he's dead." I grabbed her arm, swinging her up. I carried her into the clearing, wondering where I would run. The bodies of dead Berserkers lay where they died, marking where Samuel had been. Brenna gasped and hung onto me.

We'd almost gotten to the forest when a wind washed over us, bringing the stench of blood and tainted magic.

"Run, lass," I cried, pushing Brenna forward and turning to face the disfigured Samuel. Claws the size of knives hung down from his fur covered arms. He roared a challenge and I ran, darting away from Brenna, trying to lead him off.

It worked. The beast that had once been Samuel followed me, clawing the ground in its haste to catch me. I feinted one way, and then did it again, hoping to fool it into giving chase.

My efforts only angered the beast. The next time I darted away, it lunged and caught me. I roared in pain, the beast within me rising, turning the world red. But I couldn't go under. Brenna would be alone.

"Samuel, please," I called to the creature who had once been my friend. There was no recognition in the feral eyes.

I heard a noise behind me, soft and frightened, and turned. "Brenna, no!"

Samuel's beast raced towards the woman. She'd stepped into the clearing, exposed and unprotected. I cursed as I ran, shouting for her to hide herself. She stood her ground as the beast raced towards her—

And fell, scant feet away from catching her. The clever, foolish girl had dragged leaf covered branches over the mouth of the pit. The beast hadn't noticed until they snapped under its weight.

Samuel fell, clawing at the sides of the pits, roaring as he went. The clearing shook when he landed—the psychic force whipping the trees as if in a storm wind.

I rushed to Brenna. "Damned silly lass, ye could've been killed." I clasped her to me and kissed her hair. Samuel's beast scrabbled at the bottom of the pit, letting out a pathetic roar. With reluctance, I pulled Brenna away. "Come, lass, we must leave."

After a few steps, Brenna fought me, pulling my arm until I stopped and turned. My heart broke at the thought of leaving my friend, my one time Alpha, there to die like a rat in a trap, but I knew it was for the best. Brenna turned her beautiful, stubborn face to mine. Her hands flew as she motioned her words.

Samuel. Trapped.

"I'm sorry. We must leave him."

The pit. Save him.

"Listen to me." I cupped her face in both hands. "The beast has him in its grasp. Even if we could pull him out, he would not survive. He would kill us, and die anyway. Samuel is gone."

No. She motioned. *Save him.*

"We cannae save him. Don't you think I would if I could?"

Her hands dropped. I took her arm to pull her away, and she fought me, silently, kicking and wrestling until I took her down to the grass. I could easily carry her off, but my beast was close to the surface, and I didn't want it to rouse and hurt her. I gripped her wrists to the point of pain—she winced—and snarled. "We must leave, now. And never return."

No. No.

"I'm sorry. Weep for him, when we are far away and you are safe."

Let me go. She spoke with her hands.

"What will ye do? Waste away, weeping for him? He was my friend, too. We honor him by leaving to live our lives."

I waited until she nodded. Tears glimmered in her eyes. My fingers wrapped around her wrist as we rose and set our backs to the pit.

A mistake. As soon as my grip relaxed, Brenna tugged her arm away.

"No, lass—No!" I called after her, too late. She raced ahead of me, pausing on the rim of the dark hole, and let herself fall. Without pause, I leapt after her.

We dropped into the darkness together, and I caught her in my arms, wrapping my limbs around her to be sure I hit the ground before she did. Roots and rocks scraped my skin and the force of the fall drove the breath from my lungs, but Brenna landed on me. We rolled together, and I ended up curled around her, trying my best to cushion her fall. I felt a few of my bones snap, but magic surged through me with the pain, knitting my bones and healing my wounds. I lay twitching in breathless agony, holding my woman's weight against my bruised body and praying she wasn't hurt.

My prayers were answered when Brenna stirred. She stood up, shielding her eyes against the fine beam of sunlight. The light silhouetted her beautiful form. The fall had knocked her out, but she was unharmed. Stronger than she looks, as Samuel had said.

I remembered Samuel then. Brenna took a step towards the deep shadows on the far side of the pit, and I shackled her ankle with my fingers to stop her from going to him.

"No, lass. It's too dangerous."

Brenna knelt, checking my body. Her hair brushed my bare chest and my cock stirred to life as if we were back in our chambers, on our dais bed, and not in a godforsaken pit built to trap an insane Alpha.

There was magic down here, potent and thick as fog, swirling through my head, taking away all good sense. I needed my wits about me to fight my beast and Samuel's, to protect my beloved as long as I could.

"Why did ye do it, lass?" I wheezed, as the magic healed my broken ribs and back.

Yours. She motioned. *Forever.*

She rose again, eluding my grasp and stepping into the thick stream of light that was our last remaining connection to the outside world.

She stopped in her tracks when Samuel growled. The sound reverberated around our closed space, making my hair stand on end. I fought my way up to my side, grimacing.

Please, Samuel. I begged my former Alpha using our brother bond, but the path to his mind was severed, the splintered ends painful when they once gave comfort. Samuel was gone, and only the beast remained.

It was a mercy that the fall had probably broken him

also. At least, that is why I thought he did not attack right away.

I took a moment to glance around the earthy place that would be our tomb. The dirt was littered here and there with the tiny skulls of rats and voles—the little creatures the last prisoner probably lured into the pit to eat. I looked around for Siebold's spears, but they were missing. That was probably how Maddox had escaped, using his Berserker strength to drive the spears into the walls of the pit and climb out, hand over hand. I spared a second to curse Siebold.

Maddox had widened the bottom of the pit, also, scratching and clawing a trench around the edge. That was where Samuel lurked, a beast of shadow and magic, just the thin sunlight that dared venture this far into the earth.

It was probably for the best the three of us were trapped together, though from the set of Brenna's chin, she had no intention of dying here. Indeed, she stood in the circle of light staring towards the beast in the darkness.

When she stepped towards him again, the growl sounded and I found enough strength to rise and stagger between her and the mad Alpha.

"Samuel. We are here, brother."

His roar came with a blast of magic. I fell to my knees, fighting the change as my beast came forward. For a brief moment I wondered how the pack had fared. Had they run away, guided by Wulfgar's strength and calm? Was his Alpha presence enough to save them from madness? My thoughts scattered as the red haze of the beast claimed my vision. I saw Brenna's pale form wavering at my elbow. Beyond her, the dark stain of Samuel's blood colored aura.

Cool hands touched my skin, and I came back to myself.

"Samuel," I choked, "she's here. Our mate is here. She

wouldnae leave ye." For she was our mate, truly. Neither man nor wolf could deny it. "Ye might fight the beast, for her. For our mate."

Another growl, a savage sound. The beast did not recognize any mate.

I hugged Brenna to my chest, wondering how quickly we would die.

I heard an echo though, a sound, a sweet voice. It came from very far away, an echo in my mind. A woman calling Samuel's name. It wasn't audible, just a psychic longing. A lullaby of loss and redemption, an invitation to come home. I could almost see it, a silvery strand issuing from where we stood to the darkness where Samuel crouched, ashamed.

Come out, Samuel. The humming song said. *Come into the light.*

My hold weakened on our woman, and she left my arms to walk forward. Brenna seemed to be the only one untouched by the eerie music.

Samuel's beast roared again.

I fell to my knees, fighting the change. This is what I dreaded, our fragile beloved, caught between two evil things. But I was powerless to fight my former Alpha's call. My hands turned to claws. My back arched and spine snapped as I shifted. The ache ran through me, a burst of energy that would allow me to kill.

It would be so easy to end everything, put Brenna out of the misery of being mated to rutting beasts. It would be better this way, and quick, just a snap of a fragile neck.

No, Brenna...Our mate. I fought to remember her, her sweet, soft skin, sighs in sleep, her lying naked between us.

Come out, my love, come into the light.

As the beast took hold, my eyes adjusted to the darkness. I saw my beloved and, beyond her, Samuel cringing in the shadows. The magic was eating him alive. He was hurt, hiding himself, his savagery was the bluff of a wounded animal. I sniffed the air and scented his weakness. Fear. Longing. Like a pup for its mother. An old man for his rest.

My fingers gripped the edge of my seax—a long, wicked knife. With a grunt, I tossed it beside Brenna. She glanced down. The lullaby never ceased its silvery hum.

I wanted to lay down and die in the beautiful sound.

Brenna would be safe if I died. She had the seax. She could kill Samuel. It would be so easy.

"Brenna," I croaked, it came out more a growl. "Kill...him..."

Brenna ignored the massive knife by her feet. Instead, she took a step forward.

She knelt, facing Samuel. Her head tilted to offer her own throat in the gesture of submission we'd taught her.

Watching her, I hated myself. We'd beaten her down into a plaything for us. We'd taught her to kneel to bow and beg when we should have taught her to fight.

She stretched out her hand. The magical song increased.

A growl in the dark, a curious sound.

I bowed my head, wanting to rip out my eyes, for I could not bear to see my beloved's death. In my mind's eye, I still saw her, a woman on her knees, her arms reaching for a beast of shadows and rage.

When I opened my eyes, the beast, the monstrous shape between man and wolf, had moved into the light. Brenna had not moved.

Samuel, Samuel. Came the psychic echo. *Be at peace.*

I felt a shift within my own breast. The beast still reigned, but it was quiet, controlled. The pieces of me joined together by perfect magic, as if the poisonous taint had melted away.

Samuel Changed, like a wolf commanded by its Alpha. The wolf pushed against Brenna's hand, harmless.

Some strength comes from axes or swords, or claws and teeth. Or magic.

Some strength comes from within. A lover's love. Brenna saw the beast, and she did not run. She faced it. We'd shown her who we really were, and she'd accepted it.

I rose to my knees on the cool, dry soil. Samuel shifted again, this time into a man. The beast looked out of his eyes but when he spoke, he was all Samuel.

He bent and cupped Brenna's chin where she knelt. "You have conquered us."

12

As the moon rose over the dark earth, I reached out to the pack, calling them back from where they'd scattered. In the morning, they'd return to rescue Samuel, Brenna and I from the pit, but this night, this one magical night, was ours and ours alone.

Brenna stood in Samuel's arms, caressing his face in wonder. He pulled her up against him, and I stepped close enough to press myself against her back. She sighed and quivered between us and our questing hands. We couldn't stop touching her, running our hands down her smooth flesh, unharmed.

"You didn't run," Samuel said in awe. "You didn't run." She pressed her cheek into his palm.

We sank to the floor. I held Brenna in my arms as Samuel used a claw to split her dress from neck to knee. When it parted it released her gorgeous scent. Angling her face to mine, I kissed her, speaking my need to her through the insistent pull of my lips.

She shifted her bottom on my cock, rubbing against me even while her arms reached for Samuel. Desperate clawing need roused us—I felt lust pour through the bond, a raging passion, a flood of desire.

My fingers delved into the cleft of her bottom, even as Samuel bowed over Brenna, fastening his mouth to her center. Her legs trembled as he pleasured her. He stopped when she was on the cusp.

We take her together.

I nodded. My finger tunneled into her bottom, using her copious juices to ease its way. We would claim her ass and pussy together, driving into her with all our passion, until she understood that she belonged to us, forever.

We would never let her go.

"Aye. It is time."

Samuel lay down and set our beloved onto his thick shaft. She sank down slowly, guided by his corded arms. Strain showed on his face as he signaled me.

"Now."

Bending over her, I tipped her forward to fit my cock in her arse. She shuddered as I eased into her.

"Easy, lass." I petted her back, giving her a moment to adjust. She was tight, so tight. I could feel Samuel's member in her weeping pussy, and when I reached down to stroke her clit, I touched him, too.

Brenna arched her back, taking more of me inside her. Samuel stroked her hair back from her face.

"So good," he encouraged her. "You are a miracle."

My cock slid all the way into my beloved's rear. I moved gently, with shallow strokes, getting her used to the movement. She tensed at first, then relaxed. I kissed her fine shoulder.

"Ye please us, lass."

"Ours," Samuel claimed her mouth. "Forever."

He began to move under her, his hips rolling gently. She

rocked between us as her breath came in little pants. Samuel stroked her breasts, and I kept fingering her clit. Blood roared in my ears. The beast's hunger took hold, making me move faster. I swept her hair away from one smooth, pale shoulder, and fastened my mouth on her. My teeth scraped skin.

Mark her. The beast within spoke to me, to Samuel. *Make her yours.*

With a hoarse cry, Samuel reared up, his hips pounding Brenna as his teeth claimed her other shoulder.

Fangs grew in my mouth. My head snapped forward with need and my jaw closed down onto her shoulder. The beast was insatiable. Her blood filled my mouth.

She bucked between us, suspended in pleasure and pain. I jerked and came into her, filling her ass with my seed. Samuel came with a roar.

Brenna's head rolled back, limp with pleasure. I buried my face in her hair, tasting her sweet blood. The beast howled its pleasure as I lay down and slept.

WE WOKE in a tangle of limbs. Brenna lay between us.

I reached out to Samuel through our brother bond. The mental path lay between us, strong and secure, as if it had always been.

What happened?

The beast took hold. She survived.

My memory returned and in a panic, I pushed back Brenna's hair back to see the sort of wounds we'd marked her with. Samuel did the same, and we both touched the unbroken skin of her shoulder with wonder.

"What magic is this?"

Instead of a bloody wound, all that remained of our claiming marks were two neat sets of punctures, beautifully healed.

Samuel traced his marks on her right shoulder. "Mating bite."

"That means..." My voice choked. Mating heat, mating bond, mating bite.

She woke then, and we knew it before she opened our eyes. She was our mate now, and we were connected as if her mind linked to ours. When her eyes did open, she saw us watching from either side of her. She looked first to me, smiling as I touched her hand to my lips. Her head turned towards the Alpha, taking in his leonine features as if searching for a trace of madness. When she was sure there was none, her smile widened.

Then we heard her soft voice in our minds, clear and lovely as the clarion sound of birdsong on the morning breeze.

Hello, Samuel.

~

A note from Lee Savino:

THANK you to all who reviewed *Sold to the Berserkers* and encouraged me to write more of the Berserker series. Samuel, Daegan and Brenna's story continues in the final installment *Bred to the Berserkers*. Available (free) only to members of Lee Savino's email list. Join today by downloading the Free Book offer at www.leesavino.com.

FREE BOOK

Get a secret Berserker book, Bred by the Berserkers (only to the awesomesauce fans on Lee's email list)
Go here to get started... https://geni.us/BredBerserker

A NOTE FROM LEE SAVINO

Hey there. It's me, Lee Savino, your fearless author of smexy, smexy romance (smart + sexy). I'm glad you read this book. If you're like me, you're wondering what to read next. Let me help you out...

If you haven't visited my website...seriously, go sign up for the free Berserker book. It puts you on my awesome sauce email list and I send out stuff all the time via email that you can't get anywhere else. ;) leesavino.com

And if you want more Berserkers, turn the page for the whole list...

WANT MORE BERSERKERS?

These fierce warriors will stop at nothing to claim their mates...

The Berserker Saga

Sold to the Berserkers - – Brenna, Samuel & Daegan
Mated to the Berserkers - – Brenna, Samuel & Daegan
Bred by the Berserkers (FREE novella only available at www.leesavino.com) - – Brenna, Samuel & Daegan
Taken by the Berserkers – Sabine, Ragnvald & Maddox
Given to the Berserkers – Muriel and her mates
Claimed by the Berserkers – Fleur and her mates

Berserker Brides

Rescued by the Berserker – Hazel & Knut
Captured by the Berserkers – Willow, Leif & Brokk
Kidnapped by the Berserkers – Sage, Thorbjorn & Rolf
Bonded to the Berserkers – Laurel, Haakon & Ulf

Berserker Warriors

ALSO BY LEE SAVINO

Ménage Sci Fi Romance

Draekons (Dragons in Exile) with Lili Zander (ménage alien dragons)

Crashed spaceship. Prison planet. Two big, hulking, bronzed aliens who turn into dragons. The best part? The dragons insist I'm their mate.

Paranormal romance

Bad Boy Alphas with Renee Rose (bad boy werewolves)

Never ever date a werewolf.

Sci fi romance

Draekon Rebel Force with Lili Zander

Start with Draekon Warrior

Tsenturion Warriors with Golden Angel

Start with Alien Captive

Contemporary Romance

Royal Bad Boy

I'm not falling in love with my arrogant, annoying, sex god boss. Nope. No way.

Royally Fake Fiancé

The Duke of New Arcadia has an image problem only a fiancé can fix.

And I'm the lucky lady he's chosen to play Cinderella.

Beauty & The Lumberjacks

After this logging season, I'm giving up sex. For...reasons.

Her Marine Daddy

My hot Marine hero wants me to call him daddy...

Her Dueling Daddies

Two daddies are better than one.

Innocence: dark mafia romance with Stasia Black

I'm the king of the criminal underworld. I always get what I want. And she is my obsession.

Beauty's Beast: a dark romance with Stasia Black

Years ago, Daphne's father stole from me. Now it's time for her to pay her family's debt...with her body.

ABOUT THE AUTHOR

Lee Savino is a USA today bestselling author. She's also a mom and a choco-holic. She's written a bunch of books—all of them are "smexy" romance. Smexy, as in "smart and sexy."

She hopes you liked this book.

Find her at:
www.leesavino.com

CPSIA information can be obtained
at www.ICGtesting.com
Printed in the USA
LVHW092216140321
681555LV00027B/467

9 781648 470134